The Mistcoast Misfits

Tessa Marie

Lilac Ivy BOOKS

Published by Lilac Ivy Books
Dallas, TX

Library of Congress Control Number: 2026904833

ISBNs
979-8-9916626-2-8 (paperback)
979-8-9916626-3-5 (hardcover)

First edition 2026

To my mom, who always says that life—and family—is messy, yet never fails to create beauty out of the messiness.

If you were a cloud, then I'd be your sky
If you were the ocean, I'd sail through the night
If you were the stars, then I'd be the moon
'Cause I love you, I love you, I do

If you were a bird, then I'd be your nest
If you're ever tired, then I'll be your rest
If you're ever lost, then I'll be your route
'Cause I love you, I love you, I do

If you ever need me, then I'll be right here
So close, little eyes, there's nothing to fear
Now sleep, little child, the day will come new
'Cause I love you, I love you, I do, I do
'Cause I love you, I love you, I do

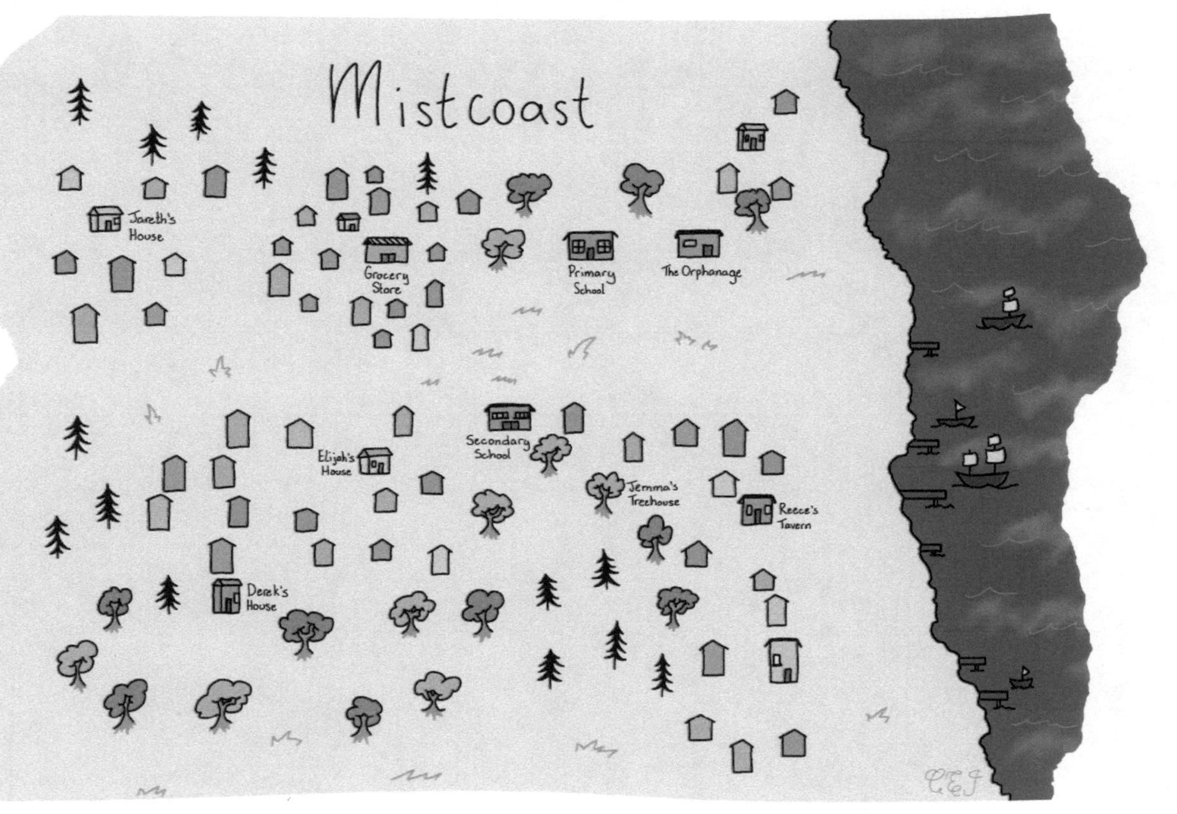
Mistcoast
Jareth's House
Grocery Store
Primary School
The Orphanage
Elijah's House
Secondary School
Jemma's Treehouse
Reece's Tavern
Derek's House

Part I

The Shore

Elijah

"Happy birthday!" Elijah hugged his son tight.

"I can't breathe, Dad!" Tobias shouted with a laugh.

Elijah let his son go. Hugs were the only gift he could afford; he had barely managed to bargain for the chocolate muffins in front of them. His son, his favorite child (albeit his only child), was turning eight today. It was a cause for celebration, as Elijah's sister Sophia had reminded him all week.

"What do you want to do today, son?" Eli asked.

"Well after school, we could—"

"I was thinking you could skip school today."

Tobias's eyes widened, and his jaw dropped. "Really?"

"Sure, kid. It's your birthday!"

Tobias ran and hugged his dad again. "No school!" he shouted in excitement.

"What do you want to do today?" Eli asked again.

Tobias took a long pause, clearly thinking through all the options. Eli began to worry. Maybe he should have set some parameters before allowing the kid to pick an itinerary.

"I know, Dad! I have an idea!" Tobias grinned. Eli knew that expression well. The kid was up to no good, about to ask to do something or go somewhere prohibited, whether a place or activity not appropriate for children or one they simply couldn't afford.

"What is it?" Eli asked, hiding his nervousness.

"I want to spend all day on a boat with you, Dad. Just me and you and the ocean"

Eli smiled. He wasn't one to cry, or even to smile much, but this kid broke him. "Yeah, Tobias. We can do that." Eli's small fishing boat was a familiar hangout spot for him and his son; he worked at the docks on the west side of Mistcoast, fishing in the morning while his son was at school and mending boats in the evening while his son ran around the shore. "It's going to take some work, though," Eli reminded him. "We'll need to get some bait, pack our lunch..."

"And dinner," Tobias said.

"Dinner? Are we staying out that late?"

Tobias grinned. "There's no bedtime on your birthday, right?"

Elijah chuckled and ruffled his son's wavy brown hair. "We'll see, kid."

With a fishing pole in one hand and his son's hand in the other, Eli headed out the door. Tobias insisted on carrying the bag of food himself, as if the weight of a few muffins and apples was a test of his strength. They followed the sound of crashing waves. "Come on, Dad!" Tobias walked faster, tugging on his father's arm impatiently.

The duo walked along the ocean past the docks, home to ships and boats of all sizes. Although Mistcoast was relatively small, the docks stayed busy at all times. The town was an entrance for traders coming to Arydia from other countries, which meant the docks hosted many different ships carrying a variety of goods. To most who entered, Mistcoast was just a checkpoint, a small stop on the way to their final destination, but to Elijah and Tobias, Mistcoast was home. Elijah knew these docks like the back of his hand—he had discovered every loose board and every hiding spot as a kid—and now Tobias had had the opportunity to grow up learning the same.

After passing the large cargo ships, they reached an area with smaller fishing boats. Docked at the end, the furthest walk from the town, was Elijah's rowboat. Technically, the boat belonged to Elijah's boss's boss, who took payments out of Elijah's pay each week, but Tobias didn't know the difference. He hopped in his dad's boat with a huge grin on his face.

"Alright, son, don't lean over the edge of the boat," Elijah warned. "I don't want to have to jump in and catch you like last time."

"I won't fall out!" Tobias promised.

"Are you sure?" Eli asked.

"I was only seven then! And now I'm eight!"

Eli chuckled as he untied the boat from the dock. "Right, you're all grown up now." He said it with sarcasm, but in a sense, it was true. It felt like just yesterday, Tobias was a little kid learning his colors and numbers, and just the day before that, he was a toddler learning to walk with his mom holding one hand and his dad holding the other. Elijah missed those days, when Tobias was younger and his mom was still around, but he was learning to cherish the present as well. He hugged his son again before he rowed the boat away from the docks, ready to catch some fish and make some memories.

Derek

"Straighten your back. Relax your shoulders."

"I'm trying," Derek said through gritted teeth.

"Try harder."

Derek released the string of his bow, sending an arrow a foot to the left of its target. "This is stupid, Torin. I'd rather be reading." He had just bought a new book on medicine that morning and only had time to finish a couple of pages before his older brother dragged him outside.

"Healing people doesn't put food on the table," Torin insisted.

"Food is useless if everyone's dead."

Torin grabbed his shoulder sternly. "You can read a boring book later. Right now, I need to teach you how to kill something." He looked at the concentric circles they had drawn on a tree. "Aim again. Stand tall. Relax your shoulders. Breathe."

Derek took a second to calm his frustration before following the instructions. He aimed the arrow carefully and nervously held his breath as he released. The tip of the arrow scraped the edge of the tree, taking a small piece of bark with it. Derek shrugged. "Better."

"Not good enough," Torin reminded him. "You'll never hit a moving target if you can't hit a stationary one. You need to work on your technique."

"We've been practicing forever, and I still can't hit the target."

"It's only been an hour," Torin said. "Keep practicing. I'm going to go find dinner." Torin headed off further into the woods.

"Can't I just go home?"

"Practice!" Torin yelled over his shoulder.

Derek begrudgingly picked up the stray arrows and wandered back to the starting line Torin had drawn in the dirt.

He shot an arrow. It missed, flying past the right side of the tree trunk.

This was stupid. It wasn't his fault that his dad was getting older and couldn't hunt with Torin anymore.

He drew the bow again with reckless speed, and the arrow flew too far to the left.

It wasn't his fault that his family didn't have food to eat.

He yanked another arrow from his quiver, and it somehow managed to hit a different tree in the distance.

It wasn't his fault that his parents decided to have nine kids.

He screamed at the woods around him as he shot the last arrow, which hit the tree, finally leaving a dent in the target he'd been aiming at for hours. It was luck, pure luck.

He retrieved the arrows, tossed them back in the quiver he borrowed from Torin, and tried again. He hated archery, but he loved his younger siblings and wanted them to have a better life than he did. If that meant learning to hunt, then so be it.

He shot one arrow after another, missing the target repeatedly. His arms began to ache from the tension of the bow. After what seemed like an eternity, Torin returned, dragging a fresh kill behind him. "Let's go home."

The small house was chaotic, full of children running amok in the cramped living room. Torin headed towards the kitchen where their mom was presumably cooking while Derek sat in the middle of the swarm of screaming children. "Derek, did you bring me back a cool stick?" six-year-old Trevor said.

"You already have too many sticks in your collection. I can't keep bringing you more sticks."

"Is it dinner time yet?" seven-year-old Nora asked.

Derek shrugged. "Torin just got home, so probably not yet. Go ask Mom in the—" Nora ran off before he finished his sentence.

Tara pushed aside some toys and sat beside Derek on the floor. Derek refused to pick a favorite sibling, but if he did, it would be her. They were closest in age, which should have caused them to fight a lot more, but raising their younger siblings together bonded them in a way most people would never understand.

"Did you kill anything?" Tara asked.

Derek shook his head. "No. I couldn't even hit the tree."

"I'm sorry." She wrapped an arm around him. "I know you hate it."

"It's exhausting," he said as he massaged his shoulder.

She leaned in close so their siblings couldn't hear. "Don't wear yourself out too much. You need your strength."

Derek chuckled. "What did you sign me up for?"

She grinned. "Just the usual, the day after tomorrow. Can I come with?" At the sound of a crying baby, her smile disappeared. She stood and walked over to pick up Alec out of his crib. The other kids yelled across the room, accusing each other of waking up the baby. "It's fine; calm down," Tara said. "He's awake now. Yelling will only make him cry more." With her son cradled in her arms, she returned to her spot beside Derek.

Derek gestured to the baby. "You can't bring him if you come with me."

"Torin could watch him," Tara joked.

Derek laughed at the idea. “Seriously, though, you’re not thinking about bringing a baby with you, right?”

“Kyla could watch him.”

Derek looked across the room at Kyla, who sat in the corner playing with a doll. “Isn’t she a little young for babysitting?”

“We were taking care of our younger siblings by her age.”

Derek shrugged. “You’re not wrong.”

Tara leaned against her brother and took a deep breath. “Do you think we did a good job?”

Derek turned to face her. “Why do you ask?”

“I don’t know.”

Derek sighed. “I think we did the best we could. We were kids taking care of kids.”

Tara shook her head. “We should have done better.”

“You’re thinking about Devin and Thomas, aren’t you?”

Tara nodded silently.

“We did the best we could.” Derek held his little sister tight, and she squeezed her son tighter. They sat in silence together as tears streamed down Tara’s face. “I miss them too,” Derek said, reading her unspoken thoughts.

“Do you think I’ll be a good mom?” Tara asked.

“Of course you will be,” Derek assured her.

“It’s so hard. I love Alec—I really do—but I wish I hadn’t had a kid so soon. I feel so bad for saying that. I feel like a bad mom for even thinking such a thing. But I really was too young to have a kid. Seventeen-year-old me was stupid.”

“Seventeen-year-old you was a rebel,” Derek said, “but eighteen-year-old you is going to be the best mom ever.”

"Kids, dinner is ready!" their mom yelled from the kitchen. The little kids sprinted towards the food. The older ones took their time, knowing the food wouldn't disappear in the seconds it took to walk to the dining room. Derek sat at the table sandwiched between Tara and Torin.

"Meet me outside again tomorrow morning," Torin told Derek. "Actually, make that every morning for now. You need more archery practice."

Tara gave Derek a look, urging him to argue, but he refused and gave Tara a defiant look back. Tara rolled her eyes. As always, Torin didn't notice their unspoken communication.

"Can we be done by early afternoon? I have plans this week," Derek said.

"What plans?" Torin asked.

"None of your business."

"Is it a date?"

"No."

Torin chuckled. "Right. You couldn't get a date if you tried."

"Torin!" Tara scolded.

"You should take lessons from Tara," Torin told Derek. "She knows a lot about getting dates."

"Shut up," Derek warned.

"She's been on a lot more dates than you, remember? First Jax, then about ten other guys we don't know the names of. I don't even think she remembers their names. Then there was Alec's dad, whatever his name was..."

Before Derek could even react, Tara handed her baby to Kyla and leapt over Derek, knocking Torin out of his chair and to the ground. She threw her fist towards his face again and again, but he dodged every attack.

Derek tried to grab Tara's shoulders and pull her off of him, but she elbowed him in the side. Trevor and Lila tried to join in the brawl, forcing Derek to focus his efforts on wrangling the kids instead of protecting Tara. After a few seconds of self-defense, Torin fought back. It only took one good hit for him to knock Tara off of him, yet he still went for a second and a third punch anyways.

"Hey, stop! Cut it out!" their mom yelled. She picked up Tegan, the youngest of the siblings, and covered her eyes. "You're scaring the kids!"

With one last successful punch to the face, Torin backed off of Tara, leaving her lying on the ground. She curled up in a ball, hiding her face against her knees. Their mom carried Tegan into the kitchen without another word. Torin stormed off into the living room, and Kyla followed behind with Alec in her arms.

Derek knelt beside Tara, trying to get a look at her injuries: a difficult task considering she was trying to hide them. He knew she didn't want the kids to see.

"Is she okay?" thirteen-year-old Caleb whispered. The kids stared at Derek and Tara on the ground, some with looks of curiosity, others with looks of horror.

"How about you all go play hide-and-seek outside?" Derek suggested. "Caleb gets to start. You have 30 seconds."

"I... um... right. Hide-and-seek," Caleb said. "Okay, I'm going to start counting." He closed his eyes. "One... two..."

Before he got to three, the kids were out of the room. Caleb took a deep breath. "Is she going to be okay?" he asked again.

Derek nodded. "I'll make sure of it. Can you distract the kids? Keep them out of our room?"

Caleb nodded back and headed outside to find them.

"They're all gone, Tara," Derek told her.

She slowly turned her head to look at him. "It hurts to move."

"I know," he said. He wrapped an arm under her back and helped her sit up, then stand. "Can you walk to my room?"

"Yeah." She limped along with his support.

His room, which he shared with three of the other boys, was an absolute mess. Sticks and rocks and toys and books covered the floor and the furniture. Derek pushed the clutter off his bed and helped Tara sit down. He crawled under the bed and found the first aid kit that he kept hidden so the others wouldn't dig through it. Once retrieved, he set it to the side and took a moment to study Tara's injuries.

Her face was covered with blood, mostly from her bleeding nose. She had a black eye as well, but that would heal with time. Derek was more worried about the cuts and bruises covering her hands.

"Open and close your hands for me."

She did as he instructed and winced in pain. He pointed to the pinky finger on her right hand. "That one hurts, doesn't it?"

"They all hurt, but especially that one," she said.

He nodded. "It looks broken."

She sighed in frustration.

"It'll heal," he promised. He cleaned the cuts on her hands and taped her broken pinky to her ring finger. "You must have hit him pretty hard," Derek said.

"I missed. I punched the floor."

Once Derek finished bandaging her hands, he moved on to assess her face.

"How bad is it?" she asked.

He showed her in a mirror. "It looks worse than it is," he promised. With a wet rag, he gently cleaned the blood off her face, then showed her the mirror again. "See? Much better."

Her shoulders dropped once he finished cleaning the wounds. "I'm sorry, Derek. I should have just let it go."

"I'm sorry he treats you like crap," Derek said.

"You should teach me to fight," Tara said with a grin.

Derek shook his head. "Nope. Absolutely not."

"Can I at least come watch you fight?"

He thought for a moment as he packed up the first aid kit. "Fine. Leave Alec with Kyla. Most importantly, don't—"

"—don't let Mom and Dad find out. I know."

Jemma

Jemma sat in her treehouse staring at the sky. Well, it wasn't really a treehouse, but it was a tree, and it was her home. Did that make it a treehouse? She wasn't sure.

"Jemma, wake up!" A pebble hit her in the side of the head.

"I'm awake! I'm coming!" she yelled.

"Hurry up!" Callum yelled back.

She jumped to the ground from a height that was borderline reckless. "Where are we going?"

He grinned. "To the tavern."

She returned the smile. "Let's go."

They crept through the alleys of Mistcoast, sticking to the shadows as if they were allergic to the light. If they were successful in their self-made game, no one would notice their passing.

Once they reached the docks, they stepped into the dim glow of dawn. The docks and nearby inns and restaurants were mostly occupied by traders and adventurers. No one but the shop owners would recognize them, and they knew one in particular who wouldn't mind their presence.

The teenagers entered the busy tavern. People packed inside, loudly occupying any empty chair they could find and often settling for standing room instead. Jemma pushed her way through the crowd, bumping into strangers as expected. Callum followed behind.

When she reached the bar on the opposite side of the room, she held up two silver coins. Callum smirked. "You're a pro at that," he said.

"It's not hard," Jemma responded. Crowds like this made pickpocketing easy. She slid the coins across the bar. "Two beers."

The bartender Reece chuckled and slipped the coins in his pocket. "Nice try, kids." He slid Jemma and Callum each a cup of apple juice.

Jemma rolled her eyes, but she didn't dare complain. Reece was the only shop owner who hadn't kicked them out for pickpocketing, although he had warned them that if they got caught, he wouldn't help them in a fight. There were plenty of altercations that occurred in this bar, and Reece only picked sides if doing so brought in profit.

"When will he give us real drinks?" Callum asked.

"When we turn eighteen," Jemma said with a sigh. She spun her chair around to watch the other patrons socialize.

"He doesn't know our birthdays. We could lie," Callum whispered.

"I heard that!" Reece shouted.

Jemma rolled her eyes and took a sip of her juice. "He knows my birthday."

"How?" Callum asked.

"Clarissa told him."

Callum leaned back against the bar. "Of course she did. I can't stand her."

"She ruins all my fun."

Callum grinned. "We could steal from her."

Jemma shook her head. "We can't. I can't do that to her."

"But you hate her!"

"I do! But not enough to steal from her. She's already broke, and everything she has goes to running her little charity. I'm a thief, not a jerk."

Callum sighed. "You're no fun," he argued, but he spoke with a tone that suggested he agreed with Jemma's call.

"Hi, Jemma," a quiet voice whispered in the young girl's ear. She spun around to see Sparrow.

"Goodness, you scared me," Jemma whined.

Sparrow shoved Callum out of his chair. "Mine." She claimed it before he could sit back down.

Callum shoved her back. "No, I was sitting there!" Despite his insistent shoving, she didn't budge. She held onto the chair with both hands wrapped under tight like it was her prized possession.

"I'm sitting by Jemma now!" Sparrow declared.

"Children!" Reece shouted. "I will kick you out of here if you don't stop with your little tantrums."

"We're teenagers, not children," Sparrow told him.

"I don't care if you're middle-aged adults," Reece said as he poured a drink. "If you act like that, you can't stay here."

"My chair," Sparrow argued.

"Fine." Callum stood beside her and leaned back against the bar.

"You two fight like siblings," Jemma noted.

"How would you know? Aren't you an only child?"

Jemma shrugged. "I've spied on the Comicus family enough. They have like twenty brothers and sisters."

The trio fell silent in anticipation as a small band stepped onto a worn wooden stage. As the upbeat folk music began to play, some people formed a circle around the open center of the floor, and others pushed their way into the middle and began to dance. Jemma watched as a small merry crowd of men and women, young and old, locals and travelers, gathered in the center of the tavern.

Callum downed the last of his apple juice, slammed down the empty cup, and held out a hand. "Sparrow, will you dance with me?"

Sparrow answered with only a look.

He took a step forward. "Jemma, will you dance with me?"

She took his hand and they joined the busy dance floor. Jemma had never liked dancing, but the activity was an effective distraction from mischief. They weaved through the dancing patrons. Everyone was smiling, enjoying the music and the company. No one would miss a small object from their pocket: a dagger, a matchbook, a few coins here and there. After only a couple of songs, Jemma had filled her satchel with a new collection of trinkets. "Let's get out of here," she whispered to Callum.

He gave Sparrow a signal from across the room, and she disappeared behind the bar. They met her outside at the tavern's hidden back entrance: a hatch in the ground hidden under leaves that led to the cellar, which was attached to the kitchen. Jemma dumped out her bag on the ground, and they took turns choosing items to keep. In theory, they were also supposed to take turns being the thief of the evening, yet most of the time, it was Jemma. After all, she was the best at it, and at least if she was caught, she'd have her two best friends to break her out of jail.

A whistle came from the woods, two high-pitched tones in an odd rhythm. Sparrow glanced back. "I have to go," she said. In typical Sparrow fashion, she disappeared as quickly as she came.

Jemma looked to Callum for an explanation, but he just shrugged. They finished splitting the loot and packed their bags.

"What else do you want to get tonight? A diamond bracelet? A new cloak?" Callum asked as they walked along the shore.

"A boat?"

"There's no way we could manage that without getting caught."

Jemma grinned. "Is that a challenge?"

They sprinted towards the docks and crouched in an alley, watching the boats and their passengers. "Which one do you want?" Callum asked.

"The biggest and fanciest ship," Jemma said.

"Do you know how to sail a boat?" Callum asked.

Jemma shook her head. "No clue. I was hoping you knew. You were on a boat once."

"Yes, as a stowaway. All I learned was how to hide."

"That's what we should do! Be stowaways on a ship! We could travel anywhere we want!"

Callum's eyebrows raised. "Really? You'd leave Mistcoast so quickly? You've been here your whole life."

"I've hated my whole life," Jemma reminded him. "Let's leave tonight. Which boat do you want to get on?"

"At least think about it for a day, Jem," Callum said.

Jemma watched the travelers move on and off their boats, loading and unloading goods. It seemed fun to sail on a boat, to see the world, to experience life outside this tiny town. The tourists always seemed so happy, but the people of Mistcoast never seemed to smile. That's why Jemma hated this place. She wanted to leave the country of Arydia and sail across the ocean to Talmar or Laresse. She didn't know much about the other nearby countries, but Clarissa said the grass was always greener over there. Jemma wasn't sure why anyone cared so much about the grass.

"Fine," she said. She didn't want to wait, but even more so, she didn't want to leave without Callum's help. "We'll wait until tomorrow."

"What are you two doing?" An accusing voice spoke from behind them.

They whipped around, daggers drawn and ready to attack. Reece took a step back. "Hey, kids. Chill. Someone in the tavern said there were two weird teenagers hanging out in the alley. I figured it was you two."

"Why did you come find us?" Callum asked.

Reece shrugged. "To tell you to get better at hiding and to tell you to get some sleep. It's late. Go home." Reece walked away before they could argue with him.

"I hate to admit it, but he's right," Callum agreed. "It's late."

Jemma nodded. "Stowaways need their sleep."

Jareth

Jareth packed his backpack with everything he might possibly need for the day: two canteens of water, a variety of snacks, and a jacket in case it got cold (which it never did). He had a long day of work ahead for a boss that rarely let him take a break, so he couldn't afford to forget anything.

"Are you leaving already? It's barely dawn," his mom complained. She sat at the kitchen table, playing a game of cards against herself.

"I have to open the store today," he explained, giving his mom a hug before heading towards the door. "I'll be back for dinner."

Jareth walked down the road as the sun emerged from the horizon. His conversation with his mom repeated in his mind. *I have to open the store today.* He had to open the store every day for the past year since he started working overtime. She just never remembered. She didn't know what day it was or when the weekend would come. Her memory was failing her, and the problem was only worsening.

This was why Jareth had to open the store. He needed the extra money from the extra hours, even though he wasn't sure what to do with it yet. If medicine existed to help with his mom's condition, it would be expensive. At the very least, he'd need someone to help him care for his mom eventually during the weeks when his dad was away on the boat, and paying for that with his grocery store salary wouldn't be easy.

At least his mom still remembered who Jareth was. He was grateful for that every day.

He unlocked and entered the grocery store. The shop was small, which meant he could run it by himself most days. He bought stock from local farmers and kept track of all the sales, hiring extra help during the busy seasons right before holidays. He could basically manage the place by himself with no oversight, if his boss would allow it.

Jareth unpacked a fresh box of tomatoes as a few customers trickled in. Some were locals he knew by name, and others were travelers he'd never see again. He greeted each one the same and happily assisted them with their shopping, all until Callum and Jemma entered.

"Are you here to steal something again?" Jareth asked with a glare.

"I only stole an orange last time," Jemma said.

"That's still stealing."

Callum handed Jareth a handful of coins. "Here. We just need some food we can take on the road, something that won't go bad if it stays in my backpack for a week."

Jareth didn't question the reason; he didn't want to know. As long as they were paying customers, they could buy whatever food they wanted. They took some potatoes and some oranges before heading out. He could have reported them for skipping school, but it wasn't worth it. They probably hadn't been to school in months. They might not even have an assigned teacher at this point.

The teenagers left peacefully with their food, and the rest of Jareth's day went by with relative quiet. As evening approached, he closed the store and headed home with a full bag of produce in hand.

"Hi, Jareth! How was your day?" his mom asked as he unpacked the bag of food in the kitchen.

"It was good, same as always," he said.

"Did you say hi to Clarissa for me?"

"She didn't come by the store today."

"Well, that's unfortunate. We should go visit her and the kids sometime. I like seeing them."

Jareth smiled. "I know." Seeing the little kids brought her a genuine bit of joy that nothing else seemed to replicate.

Once he finished unloading groceries, Jareth picked up his book and sat on the couch. He opened to the last earmarked page, the beginning of a chapter on attack spells. It wasn't his favorite class of magic, but he was determined to learn a bit of it anyways.

Most people thought that magic was inherent, a power one was born with that needed to be properly controlled. In reality, at least for Jareth, it was much more academic. It was less like learning to play a sport and more like learning to solve math equations. Every spell had a series of carefully executed steps required to produce the desired result. He stayed up late into the night, reading and rereading and studying and memorizing, taking a break only to make sandwiches for dinner. There was one attack spell in particular he was determined to master, a spell called Knife that shot a shard of energy across a room. It was one of the few attack spells in the book that couldn't cause mass destruction. It did, however, easily demolish a paper target on the wall of his bedroom and put a dent in the wood behind it.

"What's that noise, Jareth?" his mom shouted from the other room.

"Nothing, Mom!" he shouted back. Maybe this was a spell best practiced outside. He glanced out the window. It was already getting dark. He placed the book back on his shelf and decided that practice could wait until tomorrow.

He walked downstairs, where his mom was sitting on the couch in pajamas playing another game of cards. "I'm headed to bed, Mom. Goodnight."

"You're going to sleep so soon?" she asked. "Why don't you go out? Make some friends? Go do the crazy things that teenagers do."

He was hardly a teenager now—he was 19, almost 20—but he wasn't sure if his mom remembered that at the moment. "Not tonight," he told her.

"You should do something outside the house! Go on a date!"

"Maybe tomorrow," he said, although he already knew that wouldn't happen. The girl he liked had plenty of other things in life to worry about besides him. She had no clue Jareth liked her, and he was just fine keeping it that way. "Goodnight, Mom."

He walked back to his room, imagining ideas for a date that wouldn't happen and dreaming of a world in which his life looked much different.

Clarissa

"Miss Clarissa, I don't like strawberry yogurt! I wanted blueberry!"

"Miss Clarissa, I can't find my backpack."

"Clarissa, can we go to the beach after school?"

Clarissa handed Owen a blueberry yogurt and Melody her backpack. "Yes, we can go to the beach," she told Eloise.

She stepped back with a sigh and leaned against the wall. The kids sat and ate their breakfast relatively calmly with minimal whining. The day was off to a good start. It was hard to wrangle ten kids by herself, and every morning seemed like an impossible challenge, but somehow, she always managed. She glanced around the orphanage at the mess left around, toys scattered on the floor and dishes piled in the kitchen. Once the kids made it safely to school, she'd have plenty of time to clean.

She still remembered when the youngest kids were toddlers and her mom spent every morning trying to get them to sit still and eat. They weren't old enough for school, so all day was spent playing with them, and dishes didn't get done until late into the night. A trip to the beach would have been inconceivable. Now, the youngest was six and the oldest was seventeen. They were much easier for Clarissa to handle at this age.

"Alright, everyone, it's time for school! Grab your backpack and put your shoes on!" Clarissa knelt in front of six-year-old Abigail and tied her shoes. Once everyone was ready, the older kids stepped outside while Clarissa wrangled the younger kids behind them. "Remember, no detours! Eloise is in charge! Be nice to your teachers and work hard!" Clarissa shouted the same daily message at the teenagers as they walked off towards the secondary school. They were already talking and laughing amongst themselves, paying Clarissa no attention, but Eloise gave her a smile and a thumbs up.

"Everyone else, come with me," she instructed the younger kids. Luckily for her, the orphanage had been built right next to the primary school, making the daily trek a breeze. Abigail, the youngest of the group, held Clarissa's hand as they walked.

"Miss Clarissa?" Abigail asked.

"Yes?"

"I don't feel good."

Clarissa looked down at the small child staring up at her. She didn't appear sick. "Do you not feel good, or do you not want to go to school?" Clarissa asked.

"Both," Abigail said.

Clarissa nodded. "Well, why don't you go to school and see if you feel better soon?" The fake illness didn't surprise her; she had overheard Tristan teaching the other kids to pretend to be sick if they wanted to skip school. She needed to have a talk with him.

She dropped the kids off, said hello to the teachers, and received some updates about how the children were doing before heading back home. She spent the day washing dishes and organizing toys. The chores that used to annoy her in childhood were now her favorite part of the day. It was relaxing and slow, unlike the evening to come.

With a couple of hours left before school ended, Clarissa headed into town to go grocery shopping. The market on the north side of town was full of small tables set up with various goods for sale: blankets and books and bags and baked goods. Most of the shop owners recognized Clarissa and waved, and she returned the gesture as she passed. Growing up in

Mistcoast her whole life and being raised by parents who grew up here as well meant that everyone knew who she was, and everyone loved her (except maybe Jemma, but she told herself Jemma didn't count). The town of Mistcoast was her beloved home, and the people of Mistcoast were all her friends.

It was hard not to get distracted by everyone around her. She wanted to stop and talk, to ask Mrs. Ellis how her new business was going, to ask Tara how her baby was doing, but she kept on her path towards groceries. In the center of the market was a small grocery store that had been in town for as long as anyone could remember. It was owned by an older man named Mr. Campbell, whom many people in the town particularly disliked, but it was run by a former classmate of hers named Jareth, who waved at Clarissa as she entered the store.

"Hey, Clarissa! How are you?"

"Hey, Jareth! I'm doing good." She began filling her basket with fruit: oranges, apples, and of course, plenty of blueberries. The kids could eat two boxes of berries a day if she let them.

Jareth gathered items from around the store and brought them to her. She made the same meals on repeat to lessen the burden of cooking for ten kids, which made it easy for Jareth to predict what ingredients she needed. "How are the kids doing?" he asked as he packed a small bag with vegetables.

"They're doing well for the most part. They're learning so quickly. I mean, Abigail still can't tie her shoes, but we're working on it."

"Did Owen learn to listen to his teachers yet?"

Clarissa shook her head. "Of course not. He's still pretty defiant, but I'm hoping he grows out of it."

"He probably will. I was quite a mess at his age too."

Clarissa laughed. “You? Really?”

“Yes, me,” Jareth said with a grin that ruined any chance he had of Clarissa taking him seriously. “I caused all sorts of trouble.”

Clarissa’s eyebrows raised. “I don’t believe you.”

“I got expelled from school when I was nine for cutting a girl’s hair.”

Clarissa gasped. “No way! I don’t remember that!”

Jareth shrugged. “It’s true. She had her hair in pigtail braids, and I just cut one of them off. I was a mess at that age, but I turned out alright. Owen will too, especially with your help. Don’t be too hard on yourself.”

Clarissa smiled. “Thanks.” She handed him a few gold coins to pay for the food.

“No, Clarissa, you don’t owe me anything!”

“Let me pay for groceries!” She set the coins on the counter before he could argue any further and walked out the door. They performed the same dance every time, arguing over payment. Jareth was stubborn, but so was Clarissa. She wanted to pay him for the food; money had been donated to the orphanage for that exact purpose.

Clarissa picked the little kids up from school and started prepping dinner while they played. The older kids returned just as she finished cooking the day’s soup. “Everyone, sit down! Dinner is ready!” Clarissa shouted as she set a bowl at each seat at the table.

“I don’t like soup,” Owen said.

“Well, we’re having soup tonight,” Clarissa told him, kneeling down to talk at his eye level.

“I don’t want soup!” Owen yelled.

“Owen, we’re having soup tonight, so you need to—”

Her sentence was interrupted as Owen dumped the bowl of soup on her head, soaking her clothes in hot broth and leaving chunks of vegetables in her hair. The other kids gasped and stared at Clarissa, waiting to see her response. She wanted to yell and scream in anger, but he was just a kid. He was a seven-year-old boy. She couldn't expect him to act mature, could she?

She made a peanut butter sandwich in the kitchen and handed it to Owen, all while still being covered in soup. "I'm going to go shower. Eloise, can you watch them?"

Eloise nodded. "I've got it."

"Thanks. Eloise is in charge. Listen to her."

Clarissa walked to her room and sat against the wall, her face pressed against her knees. She couldn't do this. She couldn't parent ten children. She'd been trying her best to run the orphanage alone after her mom's passing. Despite everyone telling her how great she was doing, she knew she was failing. Her mom had done a much better job at caring for these kids than she ever could. When her mom passed six months ago, Clarissa knew things would be difficult, especially as the kids all grieved the loss of the closest thing they had to a mother. She expected time to heal the wounds, and she hoped she could learn how to properly raise them, yet six months later, everything felt like a disaster.

She wanted to give up, but she couldn't bring herself to leave. These kids needed someone, and she was all they had. Being with an imperfect nineteen-year-old parent seemed better than being alone.

She stood up from her spot on the floor. She couldn't leave Eloise alone in charge for too long. Besides, she had promised them a day at the beach. Canceling the activity would let them down.

She couldn't bear to let them down.

Elijah

"Can we go fishing?" Tobias asked.

Elijah shook his head. Ever since their fishing excursion for Tobias's birthday two days ago, the kid hadn't stopped begging to go fishing again.

"I have to work tonight, kid," Elijah said. He picked up his backpack. "Come on, let's go."

Tobias picked up his own backpack full of toys and snacks. Eli held his hand as they walked down to the docks together. After checking in with his boss, Cohen, Eli found the boat he was supposed to work on and set down his supplies. "Alright, Tobias. Are you going to stay with me and watch, or are you going to go run around?"

"Can I go to the beach?" he asked.

"We've been over this, kid. You can't go to the beach by yourself. It's not safe. Someone needs to be there to make sure you don't drown."

"But I'm a good swimmer!"

"You didn't even bring your swimsuit."

"Yes, I did!" He pulled a swimsuit out of his backpack. "Can I *please* go to the beach? I saw other kids down there! Why can they go and I can't?"

Elijah gazed down the shore, squinting to see the figures in the distance. Clarissa was there with the kids, splashing in the water and running through the shallow waves. She already had to ensure that all those kids didn't drown. Surely one more wouldn't be any different.

"Okay, fine, but you have to ask Clarissa to keep an eye on you, and you better be on your best behavior. Understood?"

"Thanks, Dad!" Tobias ran off as fast as his little legs could carry him.

Eli returned to his work repairing the boat. Although there weren't any leaks in it yet, there was plenty of the typical wear and tear he saw on all the boats that traveled such long distances. This was the more enjoyable part of his job. Some days he had to work hard to patch existing leaks, but today he simply had to stave off any future ones.

He walked through the maintenance checklist in his head, subconsciously humming a song to himself as he went. It took him a minute to realize what song he was singing: the lullaby Anna used to sing to their son every night. He switched to a different song and allowed the routine motions of cleaning the boat to distract him. He didn't want those memories right now.

The ship was spacious yet completely unoccupied. He assumed its passengers were off partying somewhere, enjoying their last day on land before a long journey at sea, but he didn't mind. It was easiest to work when no one was here to bug him. The ship took a few hours to finish, plus a few more hours to clean. The cleaning wasn't in his job description, but they gave him better tips when the boat looked shiny.

He packed up his supplies and stepped off the boat, hoping his boss would pay tonight instead of tomorrow, and even more desperately, hoping his son hadn't caused too much trouble in the meantime.

Jemma

"Come on, Callum, this way!" Jemma dragged him along through the alleyway.

"I'm trying! These bags are heavy!" he complained. They were each carrying three bags containing all their belongings and enough food for the long journey to Laresse.

Jemma looked in awe at the huge ship in front of them. "You said this one, right? We're going to get to ride on that?"

"Yes, that one. I checked Cohen's logs."

Jemma grinned. It was easy to choose a ship to sneak onto when Cohen documented every itinerary and left the book wide open on his desk. "To Laresse!" she declared with excitement.

"Rule number one of being a stowaway: be quiet," Callum reminded her.

"Right, we're being quiet," she whispered back.

The boat was empty; they had spied on it earlier and watched everyone get off. That would make their job easy. There was a rope ladder on the side for them to board the ship. Climbing with their heavy backpacks was an arduous task, but they managed. Callum went first, then turned to assist Jemma. As she stepped onto the boat, she froze.

"What are you kids doing?" Elijah asked.

"Well... our dad owns this boat!" Jemma blurted out.

"Seriously?"

"Yeah! We came here from Laresse one month ago, and we leave tomorrow morning to go back!" Callum chimed in.

"I'm not an idiot. I recognize you, kid." He pointed to Jemma. "I don't know your friend here, but I know you're a local."

"You're from Mistcoast too?" Jemma asked Eli, pretending to be surprised despite knowing exactly who he was. "That means we're friends, right? Cool. I'm just going to take a look around this boat." She took a step forward, but Elijah stepped in front of her.

"Get off this boat. Now."

"Come on, we're not hurting anyone!" Callum argued.

"I can't afford to get fired," Elijah said with a sigh. He grabbed two of Jemma's backpacks and tossed them off the boat. They hit the dock with a thud.

"Hey, stop!" Jemma shouted as he grabbed her last backpack. She tried to tug it out of his hands, but he won the contest of strength. It landed next to her other bags.

"Get off the boat now, and I won't tell anyone you snuck on here," Elijah said.

Callum yanked on her arm. "Jemma, let's go."

"I want to go to Laresse!" This was the only boat leaving for another country anytime soon. She didn't want to miss her chance.

"Jem, come on." Callum dragged her towards the rope ladder.

She looked back at Elijah, who was staring down at her with a glare. "You just want to ruin all my fun, don't you?" she said. "You just want to crush all my hopes and dreams."

"No. I want to keep this job so that my son can live out his hopes and dreams."

"Jemma! Let's go!" Callum yelled. She glared at Elijah, holding eye contact for as long as Callum would allow, before she finally turned and climbed back down the ladder. She picked up her bags and headed back down the dock, away from the ocean and away from her hope.

Elijah

"You're telling me that two kids just climbed on the boat."

Elijah nodded. "They were teenagers, not little kids. But I kicked them off."

"Good," Cohen said. "We can't have stowaways boarding on these docks or dumb teenagers causing any other shenanigans. It's our job to care for these boats. It'll make us look bad."

Eli nodded. "Understood."

Cohen jotted down some notes in his book. "I need you to figure out who those kids were."

"I know it was a boy and a girl, but I don't know the girl's name and I didn't recognize the boy." He thought for a second. "Actually, I'm pretty sure the boy referred to the girl as Jem."

"Then do some investigating. Figure it out. You're smart," Cohen said.

Eli sighed. This wasn't worth his time, but arguing with Cohen was futile. "I'll do my best," he said as Cohen handed him his pay for the day. Eli left the office and headed towards the beach.

Even from a distance, he could hear the kids shouting with excitement. As he got closer, he could see the kids playing in the water, splashing each other and laughing. He found Tobias in the mix, jumping over the waves. Clarissa sat in the sand and watched the kids carefully.

"Thanks for keeping an eye on Tobias for me," Elijah said as he approached.

Clarissa smiled at him. "No problem. He's a cute kid."

"He didn't cause you any trouble?" Elijah asked.

Clarissa shook her head. "None at all."

Elijah sighed in relief. He watched his son for a minute playing and laughing with the other kids before Tobias noticed him standing on the shore. "Hey, Dad!" The kid ran up and hugged his father, making Eli's dry clothes wet with saltwater.

"Did you have fun?" Elijah asked.

"Yes! Eloise gave me a piggyback ride, and I found some cool shells, and I made a sandcastle! Look!" He pointed to a misshapen pile of sand.

"That's awesome, kid."

"Are we going home now?" Tobias asked as he picked up his backpack and brushed off the sand.

"Actually... can you go play for a few more minutes? I need to talk to Clarissa."

"Okay!" Tobias happily obliged, tossing his backpack onto the sand again and running into the waves without a care in the world.

Clarissa

Clarissa kept her eyes trained on the children in the ocean waves, but tried her best to pay attention to Elijah at the same time. "Do you need something?" she asked with concern in her voice.

"I have a weird question," Eli said. "I'm trying to get the names of some teenagers I saw tonight."

Based on that information alone, Clarissa already had some names in mind.

"There was a boy and a girl. The girl had dark hair, tan skin, bright green eyes, about this tall." He held his hand up to his chest. "The boy had short blonde hair, and he was maybe a few inches taller. I didn't get as good of a look at him. He started backing up as soon as he saw me."

They were the exact troublemakers Clarissa suspected, although it sounded like the new girl wasn't with them tonight. "Jemma and Callum," she said with a sigh. "I'm sorry about them. What did they do?"

"They climbed onto a ship I was working on."

"Why?"

Eli shrugged. "My boss thinks they were trying to be stowaways since the ship leaves in the morning. That's just a theory, though. We're honestly not sure." He sat beside Clarissa in the sand. "How do you know them?"

"Jemma used to live at the orphanage," Clarissa explained, "but she left when she turned 16. It wasn't much of a surprise. She didn't get along with my mom well in the last year before she left. She kept skipping school to hang out with Callum."

"I'm sure your mom didn't appreciate that."

"Actually, at first she felt bad for Callum. He was just a kid too. When he and Jemma started getting arrested, though, she changed her mind." Clarissa sighed. "I don't know what kind of trouble they're in but... go easy on them if you can, okay?"

"I will." Elijah stood up and brushed the sand off his clothes. "Come on, kid!" he hollered. Tobias ran over immediately and held his dad's hand as they walked home together.

Clarissa wished Owen would listen that nicely.

"Hey, kids! It's time to go home!" She handed out towels as the kids left the water.

"Can we play a little longer?" Sara begged.

"Not today. It's late. The stars are already out, see?" She pointed to the twinkling lights in the twilight sky. The kids were going to be difficult to wake up in the morning.

"Fine," Sara relented, taking a towel.

The group began their trek back to the orphanage, Eloise in front, Clarissa in back, making sure none of the kids were lost on the journey. Luckily, the busy evening at the beach had burned all their energy. Getting ten kids to sleep was not a simple task, but given how exhausted they were, it wasn't as difficult as normal.

Once all the kids were dressed in pajamas and asleep (or at least lying quietly in bed), Clarissa went to her own room to reflect on the day.

Although dinner had been a disaster, the trip to the beach had been a welcome break. The kids weren't perfect (the twins, Charlette and Cosette, still had a fight over whose sandcastle was better), but for the most part, they played together nicely for the evening. Now the house was peaceful, entirely silent besides the rustling of leaves from the wind outside. She let the sound lull her to sleep.

"Miss Clarissa?"

She jerked awake. "What?"

"Miss Clarissa?" A tiny head peeked through the door.

"Hi, Cosette." Clarissa rubbed her eyes. "What do you need?"

"Something's wrong with Abigail." Her voice was meek, not panicked, but definitely scared.

"Okay, I'm coming." Clarissa followed Cosette back to the room where she, Charlette, and Abigail slept. Abigail lay in her bed, hugging her toy rabbit, whimpering as tears streamed down her face. "Abigail?"

"I don't feel good, Miss Clarissa."

Clarissa put her hand against Abigail's forehead, careful to keep her calm composure when she felt it burning hot.

"Is she okay?" Charlette asked.

"Charlette, go get Abigail some water. Cosette, go wake up Eloise. I'm going to go find help," Clarissa promised.

She knew only one person who could help with this, and she knew only one place he could be at this time of night.

Derek

Tara watched from the crowded sidelines as Derek stepped into the fighting ring. Derek wasn't sure what he thought of his little sister watching, but she was the one who organized this fight, so it felt only fair to let her watch.

When Tara had her seventeen-year-old rebellious phase (her "coming-of-age adventure", as she lovingly referred to it), she spent a month dating a guy who competed in underground fighting rings, and she accompanied him here regularly. Derek didn't discover this for a year—Tara didn't talk to him or any of their family at that time—but he was far from happy about it when he found out. In that same conversation where Tara recapped her year's worth of escapades, she casually mentioned that she was pregnant.

Derek didn't take it so casually.

He did, however, take it more casually than his parents, who freaked out and threatened to kick her out of the home minutes after being incredibly grateful for her return. Torin, likewise, blew up in anger, yelling at Tara for "adding another kid he had to feed". It was a difficult time for all of them, but Derek was determined to care for his little sister. He didn't know what babies needed, but he knew it was expensive, so he decided he needed to start saving up money. He asked her to use her connections to enter him in a fight. That was the beginning of his career as an underground fighter. He started for the money but stayed for the fun and the fame. Besides, it didn't hurt to learn how to throw a punch, especially when he lived in the same house as Torin.

People cheered from the crowd, both locals and tourists. Derek pumped his fist in the air as the announcer called his name and high-fived the nearest spectators. He had learned the game well; the more of a show he put on, the more money people bet on the fight, and the more money bet, the higher Derek's cut. That was, of course, if he won. Losing only paid him a small flat fee, and he wasn't prepared to take such a meager payout today.

His opponent entered: a young newbie named Max. This would be easy.

Derek scanned the crowd. Friends and strangers alike cheered him on. His sister smiled at him from the front row. He paused for a second when he noticed a figure in the back wearing a white dress and leaning against the wall, staring straight at him with a look of worry in her eyes.

What in the world was she doing here?

He snapped his attention back to the fight as the announcer counted down. He normally would have dragged it on for performance's sake, but the presence of the unexpected spectator distracted him. Derek left the fight with some bruises, and Max left with a black eye and a possible concussion.

He booked it through the crowd towards the figure in the white dress. "Why are you here?" he asked in a hushed tone.

"Abigail is sick, and I don't know anyone else who can help. She has a fever, and she's shaking, and Charlette and Cosette are freaking out, and—"

"Clarissa, calm down. I'll come check on her."

"Derek, they're looking for you to give you the payout," Tara said. "What are you... Clarissa?" Tara looked at her in confusion.

"Tara, Abigail is sick, and I—"

"Tara, get the payout for me. If they won't give it to you, tell them I'll get it tomorrow," Derek said.

Tara nodded. "Yeah, sure. I'll meet you back at the house."

Derek wrapped an arm around Clarissa and led her towards the door. "Let's get out of here. You shouldn't be here." He pushed her up the stairs and out of the tavern, leading her towards the orphanage. "How did you even know where to find me?" Why did Clarissa Amica, out of all people, know where the underground fighting ring was? How could she possibly know that he was a participant in it? How did she even know he was studying healing? He hadn't mentioned it to many people outside his own family.

"I... I don't remember who told me, but someone mentioned it once," Clarissa said.

"Just keep that information between us, okay?"

"I wouldn't tell anyone," Clarissa said.

"Thank you." They entered the quiet orphanage together, and Clarissa led him to a small bedroom. There were four girls inside: two twins, whom Clarissa quickly ushered out, a teenager who looked only a couple years younger than Clarissa and Derek themselves, and a little girl lying in her bed, coughing and shivering. Derek knelt beside her. "Hey, Abigail."

"Who are you?" Abigail asked.

"My name is Derek. I'm going to try to help you feel better, okay?" He placed a hand against her forehead, which was definitely warmer than normal, and looked at her throat, which gave him no hints as to what her illness could be. He tried his best to follow the normal routines that his medical books described, although he barely knew what he was doing.

"I think she has a fever," Clarissa said.

Derek nodded. "All that means is that her body is fighting off an infection."

"But what are we supposed to do?" Clarissa asked in panic. "Does she need medicine? Where do I get that? What kind? Does she need to go to the hospital? The closest one is in Caridelle, and that's so far—"

"Clarissa." Derek grabbed her arm and dragged her into the hallway, closing the door behind them so Abigail and the teenager couldn't hear. "You're going to scare her. Calm down. She probably just has a virus."

"So what do I do?"

"Isolate her from the other kids. Feed her soup and crackers and water. She'll be okay," Derek promised.

He hoped he wasn't lying.

Jemma

Jemma sat on the ground beside her treehouse, being swaddled by the tall grass that reached past her shoulders and tickled her chin. She ducked her head into the foliage as footsteps approached. No one could see her; they might figure out she lived here, and her treehouse was her best-kept secret. She dared to peek her head above the grass only when she heard Callum's voice. "Nice hiding spot."

Jemma responded with silence and a refusal to make eye contact even as Callum sat right in front of her.

"What's wrong?" he asked.

She sighed. Wasn't it obvious? She'd be stuck in Mistcoast forever, living in this treehouse or maybe in jail if she was arrested for her crimes.

"Mistcoast can be fun!" Callum promised. "The ocean is cool, and Reece's tavern is pretty awesome. Actually, if you want something new to see, I've heard there's an underground fighting—"

"I'm not allowed there."

"When has that stopped you before?" Callum took a deep breath. "Jem, one of these days, you'll learn that anywhere with people who care about..." He trailed off as a folded note floated through the air between their faces, landing in front of them. They both immediately looked up to see Sparrow in the branches above them.

"What's this?" Callum asked.

Sparrow shrugged. "A note from Ash for you two."

Jemma snatched up the note and ripped it open.

Hello Jemma & Callum,

I've heard so much about you two from Sparrow. I could use your help for a very specific task, but I need you in Illia as soon as possible. Sparrow will guide the way.

See you soon,

Ash

Ash was the leader of the thieves' guild of Illia and Sparrow's main point of contact with the guild. He'd sent Sparrow on multiple quests in the past (and Jemma had helped), but he'd never asked for Jemma directly. She jumped to her feet with excitement. "Callum, we're going to Illia!" She shoved the note in his face.

"I can't read it that close, Jem," he said with a laugh as he took the paper and held it out.

Jemma froze with tense excitement as she waited for Callum to celebrate with her.

Instead, Callum's head dropped. "Jem, we don't have the money for supplies to get to Illia, and we can't steal tents without getting caught."

"But..." Jemma sat back in the grass. She wanted to argue, but Callum was right. Once again, her hope of leaving Mistcoast was extinguished as soon as it was sparked.

She heard a jingling of coins and a heavy thud as a bag landed on the ground in front of her. "Ash sent that too," Sparrow said.

"No way," Callum mumbled as Jemma peeked into the bag. Inside were more coins than Jemma had ever held in her life.

"Yes way," Sparrow said nonchalantly as she hopped down from the branches.

Callum slowly stood. "Well, I guess let's go buy some tents."

Jemma jumped to her feet with a newfound energy. She was finally going to escape this stupid town.

Jareth

"Jareth, where is your dad? When is he coming back?" Jareth's mom asked.

He pointed to the calendar he kept on the wall and crossed out yesterday's date. "This is today." He pointed to nineteen days later. "This is when Dad comes back."

"I miss him, Jareth."

"I know." Jareth missed him too. His dad worked on a ship bringing goods from Mistcoast to Kimara, another port city of Arydia. He would work for a few weeks, come home for a few weeks, and then leave again. Jareth kept the calendar on the wall for his mom so she could see how long until he returned, but the calendar only worked if she remembered it was there.

He picked up his backpack. "I have to go to work. Bye, Mom. I love you."

"I love you too," his mom said as he headed out the door.

When he arrived at the store, three troublemaking teenagers stood waiting for him.

"Are you here to steal or buy this time?" Jareth asked them.

"To buy," Jemma said. She held up a large bag of gold coins.

Jareth sighed. "Where did you steal that from?"

"We didn't steal it!" The little thief seemed shocked that Jareth would accuse her of such a thing.

"Go give it back, or I'm reporting you for theft."

"She's not lying! We didn't steal it!" Callum argued.

The new girl—Jareth had heard rumors of her, but hadn't met her yet—stepped forward. "Unlock the store," she demanded.

Jareth shook his head and slipped the key in his pocket. "Not until you tell me where that money came from."

Mr. Campbell, the store owner and Jareth's boss, approached the arguing group. "What's going on here?"

Jareth sighed. "They have quite a bit of money, and it's suspicious. I'm not sure where they—"

"He won't unlock the store," Sparrow told Mr. Campbell.

"Let them in," Mr. Campbell insisted.

"They're criminals."

"They're paying customers," Mr. Campbell said as he unlocked the door with his own key.

Jareth followed them inside. "Sir, they stole that money from someone. We need to call the police."

"You don't know if they stole it. You're supposed to be nice to the customers, Jareth, not accuse them of crimes."

"Yes, sir." Jareth knew better than to argue with his boss. Besides, he could always report them to the police after work.

Jemma, Callum, and Sparrow gathered their groceries and handed Jareth about double what they owed. They clearly had no concept of money. "We're going to Illia now! Bye!" Jemma shouted as they ran out the door.

"See? Nice, innocent kids going on a little road trip," Mr. Campbell said. "You need to treat the customers better."

"Yes, sir," Jareth said again. He did treat the customers kindly—all except the thieves—but Mr. Campbell never listened to logical arguments. Jareth grabbed a broom and began sweeping the floors.

"Jareth, we're almost out of apples. Did you notice?" Mr. Campbell asked.

"Yes, sir. I put in an order for more."

"You need to sweep the floors too. There's dirt over here."

"Yes, sir," he said for the millionth time. The store was situated right off a dirt road. Customers tracked in dirt as they walked. That's why Jareth was already sweeping the floors before Mr. Campbell even mentioned it. He was used to this routine. Mr. Campbell mentioned something that Jareth had already accounted for, and Jareth pretended like his boss had come up with the idea himself. It was annoying, but Mr. Campbell never stayed for long. He just came for a few minutes every other day to make sure Jareth was still doing his job and to point out any presumable imperfections.

Once his boss was gone, the day went by peacefully. Jareth's job was mundane, but he honestly didn't mind it. He learned the names of the people in town, talked to travelers about foreign news, and organized records of purchases and profit. He found a sense of calmness in the monotony.

As he packed up to leave for the day, Clarissa entered the store. "Am I late? I'm so sorry I'm late. I can come back tomorrow."

"No, it's alright. Come on in." He opened the door for her. According to policy, the store should have been closed, but it didn't hurt anyone for him to keep it open an extra few minutes.

"I'm so sorry. I have to pick up the kids from school soon," she said as she frantically shoved groceries in a bag. "I was home with Abigail all day, and I had to find someone to watch her while I came to get groceries. She won't eat anything, so I'm trying to get some of her favorite foods and some soup—Derek said to give her soup." Clarissa scanned the list in her hands over and over again.

"Is that your grocery list?" Jareth asked her.

She nodded. "Yeah. Do you have more onions?"

Jareth held out his hand. "Here. Let me take the list. Go pick up the kids from school, and I'll bring the groceries to the orphanage."

"You'd do that for me?" She smiled and gently passed him the list.

He nodded. "Of course. It's no big deal."

She sighed in relief. "Thank you so much, Jareth." She gave him a handful of coins and headed out the door.

Jareth added the coins to a small red pouch hidden in a drawer of the checkout counter, the same place he put all of Clarissa's payments, before going through the list one by one and collecting the items she needed. He threw in some extra blueberries for her too. With the groceries in his hands and the red pouch of coins in his pocket, he headed out the door.

He walked through the market, ignoring the vendors trying to sell him their wares, and passed the primary school, waving at the kids on the playground waiting for their parents. When he reached the front door of the orphanage, he closed his eyes, took a deep breath, and knocked.

Eloise answered. "Hey... um... uh..."

"Jareth," he supplied.

"Right. Don't you work at the grocery store?"

"Yeah, that's me."

"...what are you doing here?"

He held up the bags of groceries. "These are for Clarissa."

"Jareth, is that you?" Clarissa shouted from inside. "Eloise, let him in!"

Eloise stepped aside and allowed him to enter. Clarissa was knelt down on the floor, being screamed at by a young boy. She sighed. "Jareth, this is Owen. Owen, this is Jareth."

"Miss Clarissa won't give me more chocolate."

Jareth started to reach in the groceries until Clarissa gave him a look. "He doesn't need more chocolate. He's already had enough. Jareth, can you just set the groceries in the kitchen for now? I can put them away later."

Eloise pointed him towards the kitchen, and he set the grocery bags down. "Does she want help with Owen?" Jareth asked.

Eloise shook her head. "It's okay. We're used to it. He's always a mess like this."

Jareth stepped back into the main room, unsure of what to do. He wanted desperately to help, but he didn't know how. He stood awkwardly in the doorway until Owen stormed out of the room and Clarissa walked over to him.

"Thanks for bringing the groceries."

"Is there anything else you need? I could stay for a while," he offered.

She shook her head. "It's okay. I've got it handled," she said as she walked off.

He felt bad for leaving, but he didn't know how to help. As he left the orphanage, he passed the small donation box on the outside wall and, as was his secret routine, dumped the red bag of coins inside the box.

That was the least he could do.

He walked down the main road and headed home, passing people on their way to the docks. He was stopped by Elijah and his son; he recognized them from their visits to the store.

"Hey, Jareth, right?" Elijah asked.

Jareth nodded. "Right, that's me."

"Have you seen Jemma and Callum? I heard someone saw them in the market today."

Jareth sighed. What kind of trouble had these kids gotten themselves into? "Yeah, I saw them."

"Do you know where they are?"

"On their way to Illia." Jareth couldn't tell if Elijah looked annoyed or relieved. Maybe it was both. "Why do you ask?"

"If they left town, then it doesn't matter now. Thanks for the information." Elijah said before wandering off.

Jareth continued on his way home. Today had been a surprisingly interesting day for a grocery store cashier.

"Hi, Jareth! You're home late," his mom said.

He nodded. "I was helping out Clarissa with something."

"Oh, I love Clarissa. She's such a sweet kid." Clarissa wasn't a kid by now, but he didn't correct her. "When will your dad get home?"

He walked over to the calendar and explained again. His responsibilities at home had become just as repetitive as his day job.

Elijah

"What do you mean they're headed to Illia?" Cohen asked.

"That's what Jareth said," Eli told him. "They won't cause trouble anymore if they're not here." Tobias tugged on his hand impatiently. Eli squeezed his son's hand. "Hold on, kid. Just a second." He turned his attention back to his boss. "Do you have a job for me tonight?"

"Sorry, not tonight," Cohen said. "Come back tomorrow."

Eli left the office, both grateful for the time off and annoyed at the lack of income. He hadn't had a great day fishing, so he had been hoping to get some money tonight from boat repairs.

"Dad, can we go home now?" Tobias asked.

"Do you want to go to your Aunt Sophia's house?" Eli asked.

"Yes!" Tobias shouted in excitement.

"Good. Let's see if she's free."

Elijah felt bad ditching his son for the night, but at the same time, he needed a break. He spent every minute of every day working, trying to financially provide for the two of them while raising Tobias on his own at the same time. He told himself that dropping Tobias off with Aunt Sophia was for his own good; Tobias could always use another trustworthy adult role model in his life, and Sophia, a primary school teacher, was a great one. Still, the guilt simmered in the back of his mind.

Tobias ran ahead of his dad, knocking on Aunt Sophia's door before Elijah had even reached the porch. "Hi, Aunt Sophia!" He screamed and hugged her as she opened the door.

"Hi, Toby!" Sophia hugged him back.

Elijah smiled at his sister. "Can you watch him for the evening?"

"Sure." She covered Tobias's ears as she hugged him. "You're not going to come back drunk, right?"

Elijah rolled his eyes. "You'll never let me live that down."

"That's what sisters are for!" she shouted as he walked away.

It was one time—a single time he came to pick up Tobias while drunk—but his sister had never forgotten it. He knew his reason didn't excuse his actions, but it was as good of a reason as one could have: his wife had disappeared that day.

Elijah entered the tavern with the fewest customers and kept his head down to avoid familiar, talkative faces. He wasn't in the mood for conversation. Once he had his drink, he walked back outside and sat on the edge of an empty dock, listening to the sound of the crashing waves. The moonlight reflected on the water, rippling across the ocean's surface. He reached a hand off the edge of the dock and dipped his fingers in the water. Something about it was relaxing, peaceful in a way that words couldn't begin to describe. It brought back memories of his childhood: running along the docks (and falling off a time or two), swimming and playing at the beach multiple times a week, and finding any possible excuse to ride on a boat. He thought of the long nights spent on these docks, talking with the cute girl, who later became his girlfriend, then his fiancée, then his wife. They would watch the waves together, reminiscing about the past and dreaming of the future.

Elijah looked down at the splintered wood beneath him. He had been sitting in this very spot when he found out he was going to be a father.

With an empty glass in his hand, Elijah headed back to his sister's house to pick up his son. Missing his wife wouldn't bring her back. Tobias was all he had left of her; it was best to focus on him.

Clarissa

"I don't feel good, Miss Clarissa."

Clarissa held Abigail curled up in her lap and stroked her auburn hair. "I know."

Derek had told her to keep Abigail isolated from the other children, but it was impossible to keep her isolated from Clarissa herself. She had tried at first to leave Abigail alone, visiting her room only to check on her and bring her food, but after lots of tears, Clarissa caved. Abigail feared her own illness, and she needed Clarissa to comfort her.

Clarissa wrapped the child in a blanket, singing soothing songs that her mom used to sing around the house. She comforted the girl the best she could, but she didn't know if it was good enough.

She heard a scream from upstairs: one of the boys, presumably in his room if he had listened to her instructions to go to bed. "I'll be right back," she whispered to Abigail before laying the swaddled child in bed and heading up the stairs.

The boys were in the hallway—not their room, of course—wrestling each other on the floor. Owen and Tristan tackled each other while Isaac, the oldest of the three, stood and watched. Hearing the commotion, the girls flooded the hallway as well. Clarissa tried to pull the boys apart, getting beaten and bruised by tiny fists in the process. Eloise tried to usher the girls back to their room, but they didn't budge, their eyes trained on the chaos of the fight. Finally, the two boys wore themselves out and backed off of each other.

"Owen hit me first!" Tristan accused.

"No, Tristan hit me first!" Owen shouted at Clarissa.

She glared at the boys. "You're supposed to be in bed. Go to sleep."

"But—"

"I don't care who hit first," she said in pure exhaustion. "Go to bed."

The kids wandered off back to their own rooms. Clarissa turned the corner to walk down the stairs and saw Abigail standing at the bottom, clutching her plush rabbit tightly.

"What happened?" Abigail asked.

"Everyone is okay," Clarissa reassured her as she came down the stairs. She held the girl's hand and took a few steps towards her room before she heard a knock at the front door. She sighed.

"Who's that?" Abigail asked.

"I'm not sure," Clarissa said. "Go to your room. I'll handle it." She wasn't sure she wanted to know who it was. Anyone sane should have been asleep at this time of night.

She opened the door. Derek waved at her. "I brought Abigail some medicine."

"Hi, Derek." She let him in and led him towards Abigail's room. "You're lucky you didn't come a few minutes ago. Owen and Tristan were fighting."

"Were they any good?" he asked.

Clarissa stopped walking to glare at him. "They're children, Derek."

"It's a fair question."

Clarissa rolled her eyes. "Did you say you have medicine for Abigail?"

He handed her a vial of liquid and a small measuring cup. "She's supposed to drink one of those little cups a day."

"How am I supposed to get a six-year-old to drink medicine?" Clarissa mumbled under her breath. She set the medicine in the kitchen and filled up the measuring cup, then grabbed some juice out of the cabinet and poured that in a glass as well.

Derek stood back and watched her work. "Do you want me to leave?" he finally asked.

She shook her head. "No. I want you to come with me." She took the medicine and the orange juice into Abigail's room. "Hey, Abigail."

The little girl sat up in her bed. "Hi, Miss Clarissa. Hi... I forgot your name."

Clarissa grinned. "His name is Derek."

"You're the guy who helps people feel better, right?"

"Yeah, that's me," Derek said. "The feel-better guy."

Clarissa chuckled. She could have used the moment to teach Abigail what a doctor was, but this was cuter. Besides, she wasn't sure if Derek qualified as a doctor anyways. "I have some medicine for you, Abigail," Clarissa said. "It's going to help you."

"It will?" She looked to Derek for confirmation.

"Probably," he said. Clarissa gave him a look. "Well, as long as she's not allergic to it or something. That would be bad."

"Am I allergic?" Abigail asked in panic.

"No, no, you're not," Clarissa assured her, although she had no way of knowing. She handed Abigail the medicine. "Drink this."

Abigail obeyed, barely managing to force herself to swallow it. "That's gross!" she shouted, but Clarissa was already a step ahead, shoving the glass of juice in her hands. Abigail drank the orange juice eagerly to mask the taste of the medicine.

"Take that once a day," Derek told her.

"It's disgusting. I don't want to."

Clarissa scooped up Abigail cocooned in her blanket and set her in her lap. “Part of growing up is doing things we don’t want to do.”

Derek

Torin watched as his little brother loosed one arrow after the next. The first brushed the right edge of the thin tree, the second went a little high, but the third hit its mark. Torin grinned. "Good job."

"Can we be done for the day?"

"Are you tired already?" Torin asked.

"I was tired before we even started."

"Let's go hunting."

Derek sighed, making no effort to hide his disdain.

"Fine, don't come," Torin said with a shrug, shouting over his shoulder as he walked away. "Then you and Tara aren't getting any of whatever I kill for dinner."

"Okay, fine, I'll come." Derek jogged to catch up. He couldn't care less if he didn't get dinner, but he couldn't watch his sister starve. "Seriously, you don't need to drag Tara into this."

"You two are adults. You should take care of yourselves."

"We've been taking care of ourselves and six younger siblings for years."

"And what do you think I've been doing?" Torin asked sarcastically.

"I don't know. You're never home."

"Exactly." Torin acted as if his meaning was obvious, but Derek had no clue what message he was supposed to take from his brother's sarcastic remarks.

They hid in a tree together, waiting and watching in silence. Derek hated hunting, but this was his favorite part, when his brother, for once in their lives, finally shut up. He enjoyed the silence for a long while until a deer finally came into view. Torin motioned for Derek to shoot. Derek nocked an arrow and drew his bow slowly, silently, remembering what his older brother had taught him. He worried the deer would hear his pounding heartbeat. Torin raised his bow as well, and on his signal, they both released their arrows. To Derek's surprise, he hit it, although Torin's arrow was the one to truly kill the creature.

Torin patted Derek on the shoulder. "See? You're getting better." He hopped down from the tree and walked towards the dying animal. "You can go home. I'll meet you there."

Derek paused. "You don't want me to help?" He couldn't believe his brother was passing up an opportunity to make him work.

"No, I can handle the deer. Besides, you're probably tired. You were out late last night. Did Tara finally get you a date?"

"No, I was out late helping this girl, and—"

Torin laughed. "A girl? I was joking about the date thing; I didn't think you'd really—"

"A child, Torin." Derek clenched his fists. "I was helping one of the kids at the orphanage. She's sick. She needed medicine."

Torin rolled his eyes. "Why are you so obsessed with this healing stuff? I wish I could burn all those books of yours."

"Because unlike you, I care about people. I want to help people."

Torin walked back towards Derek, step by step slowly until their faces were inches apart. "I want to help people too. Caleb and Kyla and Gavin and Nora and Trevor and Tegan; I care about them too. Medicine is useless if everyone starves to death." He stormed off towards the deer.

Derek headed back home. It wasn't worth arguing with someone who didn't even like books.

Jemma

About twenty-four hours into her journey, Jemma decided she hated walking. Traveling wasn't the fun adventure everyone presented it to be. The physical movement wasn't too bad, but the mental boredom was miserable. She and Callum had played every game they could think of, then repeated those same games dozens of times. The monotony was killing her, and by Callum's constant yawning, she assumed it was killing him too.

Sparrow, on the other hand, seemed unphased. She walked, and walked, and walked some more. She barely said a word as they traveled together, speaking only when she felt the need to inform them of something, like what kind of tree they were walking beside or a random fact about the setting sun. Callum had tried to fill in the silence with stories of his childhood in Talmar and his stowaway adventures, but eventually, even Callum was tired of talking. They traveled in silence instead, their only audible accompaniment the dirt shifting under their boots and the birds calling from the trees.

"Are we almost to Illia?" Jemma asked Sparrow.

"It takes several days," Sparrow said.

Jemma dragged her feet along the road, one foot after the other. Every step was one step closer to Illia and further from Mistcoast. She watched small creatures scurry through the grass and birds fly overhead. She wished she could fly like those birds. They could probably reach Illia in a day. It didn't seem fair that humans didn't get to fly. Even Sparrow, who shared a name with the birds, was confined to the ground.

"Sparrow, where did you get your name?" Jemma asked.

"I picked it out."

"You named yourself?" Callum asked. "Isn't that your parents' job?"

"They gave me my real name," Sparrow replied.

"What's your real name?" Callum asked.

Sparrow shook her head, refusing to give an answer.

Callum sighed. "But I want to know!"

Sparrow responded with silence and stared ahead at the path.

"I bet it's something boring. Like Susan," Callum said with a grin, receiving the glare from Sparrow that he was looking for.

"Are we just allowed to make up our own names?" Jemma asked.

"That's what most people in the thieves' guild do, unless they get given a nickname first. If the thieves' guild gives you a nickname, you're stuck with it whether you like it or not."

Jemma looked at Callum. "Should we come up with fake names before we get there?"

"Yes!" Callum shouted with excitement. "I want to be—"

"They already know your real names," Sparrow interrupted. "You don't get nicknames."

"That's no fun," Callum said. He kicked at the rocks on the road.

The sun disappeared and the stars illuminated the sky as they walked and walked and walked some more. Finally, Sparrow let them pause for the night. They set up their new tents for the second time, building them only marginally faster than the first, and climbed inside to sleep. Jemma closed her eyes and dreamed of Illia: the end to her boredom and the beginning of a new chapter of adventures.

Elijah

"Dad, I can't sleep."

Elijah felt tiny hands shake his shoulders. "Tobias, it's too late for this," he said. "Go back to bed."

"But I can't sleep!" Tobias argued. He climbed into his dad's bed.

Elijah sighed. "Okay, son. You can stay here, but you have to actually go to sleep. You have school in the morning."

"Can I skip school and go fishing?" Tobias asked.

"No," Elijah said. He was beginning to regret letting Tobias skip school on his birthday.

"How about next week?"

"Still no. Goodnight, Tobias. Go to sleep."

"Goodnight, Elijah." Tobias giggled and hid his face under the blanket.

"Did you just call me by my first name?" Eli asked with a laugh.

"No, I didn't do that!" Tobias said. He tried to hold back his laughter, his clear tell that he was lying, but he couldn't stop giggling.

Elijah hugged his son tight. "Goodnight, son."

Tobias's laughter calmed down after a minute. "Goodnight, Dad."

Eli closed his eyes, enjoying the few minutes of sleep before he was awoken again.

"Hey, Dad?"

"What is it, Tobias?"

"Can you sing that song that Mom used to sing?" Tobias asked.

"I'm not a good singer," Elijah protested. Still five years later, Tobias remembered. He'd been singing it since the day she went missing. Elijah had expected the kid to forget over time, but somehow, the song always stuck with him, etched in his memory forever.

"Please, Dad?"

"No." Elijah refused. He didn't want to hear the lullaby in his own voice. As of now, when he remembered it, he still heard it in hers. "Goodnight, son. I love you."

Tobias curled up in his dad's arms. "I love you too."

Jareth

Sleep was an illusive, mysterious concept. It was somehow not considered a form of magic, yet it followed fewer rules of logic than most magic did. Humans needed to lie down mostly still for about a third of their life while their brains invented imaginary stories to entertain them; otherwise, they felt absolutely exhausted, even to the point of sickness. That was how Jareth felt as he tried to stay awake and learn magic. The invisibility spell was confusing and complicated. Just like sleep, it made no sense. How was he supposed to make something look like nothing?

He cast the spell again, then looked at his own hand. He was still fully visible. He sighed in frustration. This clearly wasn't working, or was it? Was he supposed to be able to see his own hand if he turned himself invisible? The rules of the spell weren't defined on the page. The book simply gave names of spells with step-by-step instructions, and finding the rules and limitations of the magic was left as an exercise for the reader.

Maybe he was invisible to everyone but himself. The only way to find out was to find other people and see if they noticed him. At this time of night, Jareth knew only one place to go.

He snuck past his mom's room, hoping not to wake her up, not because she'd care that he was leaving the house but because he didn't want to interrupt her sleep. After all, she'd been encouraging him to get out of the house and socialize more, although this probably wasn't what she had in mind.

He walked east towards the docks, towards the sound of music and laughter. He found the only tavern still open and entered into the crowd, watching for people's reactions. They didn't seem to mind him, but they definitely saw him. Apparently, he still had some work to do on the invisibility spell.

He sat at a table in the back and opened the book, searching for his mistake but failing to find it. He sighed, exasperated. Why didn't the spell work? What had he done wrong? With a deep breath, he flipped to the back of the book, staring at the title page of the chapter on healing spells and reminding himself of his end goal. These were the hardest spells in the book. He needed to build up his skills first by mastering some easier spells, like invisibility. He channeled his frustration into motivation and flipped back to the spell he was working on.

"Do you want anything to drink?" someone asked.

"No, thanks," he said. He was too concentrated on the book to even look up at the person in front of him.

"Invisibility spell. You picked a hard one. Good luck," the bartender commented as he walked off.

It took a moment for Jareth to register the implications of his words. "Wait!" he called, barely catching the bartender before he disappeared into the crowd. "Do you know magic?"

The man shrugged. "A little. Why?"

"I don't know. I'm just struggling with this spell."

"Who's your teacher?"

Jareth held up his book. "I've been learning from this."

The man chuckled. "You're trying to learn magic without a teacher?"

Jareth nodded slowly.

"Learning magic on your own is nearly impossible. You need a mentor."

"And how do I find one of those?"

"You won't in Mistcoast," the man said. "No one here cares about magic. They care about building and fishing and trading, whatever puts food on the table and a roof over their heads. I've seen a few books like yours, but I haven't met anyone who lives here who's actually learning magic."

"Can you teach me?"

The man shook his head. "I can't be your mentor. I learned a little magic when I was a kid in Caridelle. I really don't know much." He started to walk away but hesitated. "I could at least give you a few tips on the invisibility spell, but then I need to get back to serving drinks." He sat down at the table across from Jareth. "What's your name?"

"Jareth Amans."

"Nice to meet you, Jareth. I'm Reece."

Clarissa

Abigail lay in her bed, curled up under two blankets. Her toys sat abandoned in the middle of the room. Her rabbit had fallen off the edge of the mattress, leaving her alone on her bed, which she hadn't moved from in two days. She had been taking the medicine for over a week, and although her symptoms had seemed to subside for a day or two, the effects were short-lived, and her condition continued to worsen.

Clarissa sat on the floor against the wall, tears streaming down her cheeks. "I don't know what to do for her. I gave her the medicine, just like you said, and I fed her soup and plenty of fruits and vegetables. I kept her hydrated and rested and... what else am I supposed to do?"

Derek placed a hand on her shoulder. "It's not your fault. You're doing everything right, Clarissa."

"What do we do now?" Clarissa was willing to do anything to make sure this girl recovered.

Derek took a deep breath, hesitating before answering her question. "Nothing."

Clarissa turned and looked at Derek in shock. "Nothing isn't an option. We have to do something."

"I don't know anything more about healing, Clarissa, and there's not a professional doctor closer than Caridelle."

"Then we go to Caridelle," Clarissa declared. She wasn't sure why the solution wasn't as obvious to Derek as it was to her.

"But—"

A knock at the door interrupted Derek's thought. Eloise peeked inside. "Jareth is here."

Clarissa and Derek stood up and quietly snuck out of Abigail's bedroom and into the chaos of the main room. The kids ran around screaming. Owen and Tristan were fighting each other again while the twins watched. "Hey, stop that!" Clarissa yelled across the room. The kids paid her no mind. She kicked away the toys blocking the door and opened it to see Jareth standing with bags of groceries and a smile. "Hey, Jareth. How are—"

The sound of glass shattering echoed through the room.

"That was Sara!"

"It wasn't me! It was Isaac!"

Clarissa closed her eyes and took a deep breath. "I don't care who it was. Stay away from the glass so you don't get hurt." She grabbed a broom and began sweeping up the glass. Derek led Jareth towards the kitchen.

"Miss Clarissa, I promise I didn't break that!" Sara approached Clarissa as she gathered the broken shards on the floor. "It was Isaac. He—" She screamed as she accidentally stepped on a piece of glass.

"Sara, I told you to stay away from that! Derek!" Clarissa shouted his name but heard no response. "Eloise!" Maybe she could fetch Derek for her, but she didn't respond either. "Sara, just stay right there." Clarissa finished sweeping up the glass and rushed to the kitchen. Jareth, Derek, and Eloise all turned to look at her as she entered.

"Sara stepped on a piece of glass. Derek, can you look at her foot?"

"These kids are going crazy," Derek said. "They need some attention. They need structure."

"I'm trying my best," Clarissa said calmly.

Derek shook his head and went to check on Sara.

"I'll go too," Eloise said quietly. She kept her head down as she followed Derek out of the room.

"Thank you for bringing the groceries again," Clarissa said to Jareth.

Jareth smiled at her. "You're welcome."

"I'm sorry about the kids. It's difficult to handle all of them and be with Abigail at the same time."

Jareth nodded. "I know you're trying your best. No one expects you to be perfect."

"It's just that Owen is still going through this defiant phase, and the twins are picking up some of his habits. Tristan learned some words at school that he shouldn't know at age ten. Then there's Sophia and puberty..." Clarissa laughed. "No one taught me how to handle that."

"Clarissa—"

"And I need to take Abigail to Caridelle. Traveling to the capital with ten kids won't be easy."

"I think you should leave them here," Jareth said.

Clarissa shook her head. "That's not an option. They can't take care of themselves, and no one is going to want to take care of nine kids."

"Then you find nine people willing to take care of one kid," Jareth recommended.

Clarissa shook her head again. "No one is going to let me temporarily dump a child with them."

"I was thinking more permanently," Jareth said carefully.

"What?"

"Well, Derek and I were talking—"

"You were talking about me," Clarissa said under her breath.

"—and we think it would be good to try to find other homes for these kids."

Clarissa stared at the ground. She had failed. She had tried her best to raise them on her own, and she had failed.

Jareth gently placed a hand on her arm. "No one expects you to be able to care for ten kids alone, Clarissa."

"My mom did it," Clarissa said.

"Your mom was a lot older than nineteen, and your mom had help. She had you."

"I have help. I have Eloise."

"Eloise graduates this spring," Jareth reminded her.

Clarissa shook her head. "I can't abandon them."

"You're not abandoning them," Jareth said. "You're helping them. You're giving them the best life you can."

"No one is going to want to take in these kids anyways," Clarissa said. "My mom already tried that, back when they were orphaned in the first place, and no one would do it."

"Things were different back then. Everyone was grieving. Everyone was trying to piece their lives back together. Do you remember what it was like?" Jareth asked.

Clarissa remembered it more vividly than he could imagine. She wished nothing more than to forget the events of that day. "I remember."

"Mistcoast is different now. It's healing. There might be people willing to adopt these kids."

"I... I need to think about it. Thanks for bringing the groceries." She walked through the chaos of the main room, where the kids were running and screaming and arguing, and entered Abigail's little sanctuary. She sat on the floor against the wall. She hated the chaos of this house. She hated Mistcoast for not having any doctors. She hated Jareth and Derek for talking behind her back, and she hated the universe for taking her parents from her.

Above all, she hated herself for failing her only goal in life.

Jareth

"So, how was your day?" Reece asked.

"Long." Jareth sighed as he pulled up a chair to the bar.

"Did you have to work late today?"

"I brought Clarissa groceries after work. I just left the orphanage a minute ago."

Reece chuckled. "You know, I've only ever heard bad things about that girl."

Jareth shot him a confused look. "That's surprising. Everyone loves Clarissa. I can't think of a bad thing to say about her." She was a bit of a local celebrity, known for helping anyone in any way she could. She had her flaws—she worried too much, and she put too much weight on her own shoulders—but Jareth couldn't think of a genuine reason someone would dislike her.

"I've only heard about her from Jemma."

"That explains it," Jareth said.

"What's the history between the two of them anyways?"

"Jemma lived at the orphanage. She turned sixteen a month after Clarissa's mom passed away. They had a rule that you could leave once you were sixteen, but they never kicked anyone out. Clarissa was trying to walk in her mother's footsteps with lots of rules and strict curfews, and Jemma didn't like that."

"That doesn't surprise me," Reece said between sips of his drink.

"All I know is that Jemma left the orphanage on her sixteenth birthday before Clarissa even woke up."

“That explains a lot,” Reece said. He tossed his empty cup aside and grinned. “Well, are you ready to learn some magic?”

“Is that why you told me to meet you here?”

“You won’t have much luck learning the shield spell on your own.”

“I thought you weren’t going to mentor me,” Jareth remarked. For a week now, Reece had been insisting he wasn’t Jareth’s mentor; he was simply “giving him a few tips”.

“It’s going to be hard to learn the shield spell by yourself.” Reece stepped away from the bar. “We’ll have to go out back for this one. There’s not enough room inside here.”

With a grin, Jareth tailed his new mentor outside.

Derek

"Good shot," Torin praised, patting his little brother on the back and looking at the arrows embedded near the center of the target.

Derek still didn't like hunting, but he did like succeeding. Seeing his progress at something he disliked was strangely satisfying, and it was nice to see his older brother proud of him for once.

"Should we head back home now?" Torin asked. "We have to get back so you can say hi to Tara before you sneak off again."

There it was. Torin couldn't compliment Derek without attacking him too.

"I'm sorry for having a life," Derek retorted.

"Will you at least tell me where you leave to all the time?"

Half of his recent escapades were fighting gigs, and the other half were visits to Clarissa and Abigail. He was only willing to tell his brother about one of those two events. "One of the orphanage kids keeps getting more and more sick."

Torin rolled his eyes. "We have enough kids at our house to worry about."

"If I can help, I want to help."

"Then help your family," Torin argued.

Torin would never understand. Derek would do anything for his family. He learned to hunt so that they could eat. He came home with bruises from fistfights so that they had clothes and toys. He taught Kyla how to read and Lila how to tie her shoes. He let Caleb cry in his arms for days when their brothers died. Torin was never home to see anything Derek did for the family.

Derek skipped dinner that night, taking the time to sit in his room and wrap his fists in preparation for the fight. Tara watched from the doorway, holding her baby in her arms. “Can I come tonight?”

Derek shook his head. “You don’t want to.” The guy he was going up against was undefeated, which meant no one wanted to fight him, which meant Derek would get paid well even if he lost. It also meant Derek would probably come home with a black eye and a broken nose. He didn’t want Tara to watch that.

After finally coaxing his younger siblings to sleep, he snuck out the window and headed towards the docks. When he entered the basement, the enthusiastic crowd parted to let him in. His opponent stood in the fighting ring with a grin. “Let’s get this over with,” Derek muttered under his breath. He imagined Torin’s face on the guy as he threw the first punch.

Elijah

"Tobias, wake up."

"I don't want to."

"Tobias, you have school!" Elijah shook him awake.

Finally, slowly, Tobias rolled out of bed. "I wish I could sleep more."

Elijah nodded. "Me too, kid."

He helped his son get dressed for school as he prepared for work. It was a lot easier now than it had been when Tobias was younger, when he couldn't put a shirt on by himself or pack his own backpack. Elijah had now become more of a supervisor than a driving force in Tobias's morning routine.

The pair walked down the path together to the school. Tobias held his dad's hand tight, and Eli looked down at his son, savoring the moment. There would be a day when Tobias outgrew this, when he could walk to school on his own and refused to hold his dad's hand, but for now, Elijah savored every moment.

"What do you think you'll learn in school today?"

"I don't know. They write the schedule on the chalkboard, but none of us can read it," Tobias said.

"Well, maybe you'll work on reading today."

"We're reading a book as a class!" Tobias exclaimed. "It's about a boy who fights dragons!"

Elijah grinned. "That sounds cool."

"Do you think I could fight a dragon one day?"

Although he had heard plenty of stories, Eli had never seen a dragon, but he didn't want to ruin Tobias's fantasies. "I think you'd be great at fighting a dragon."

"It would be awesome! I could have a super cool sword and go like this!" He mimed swinging a sword in the air.

"But you know, even if you never kill a dragon, you're still pretty awesome. I'm still super proud of you."

Tobias paused along the path with the look in his eyes that he had when he was thinking, a look that Elijah knew too well. In a quiet voice, Tobias asked, "Do you think Mom would be proud of me too?"

Elijah knelt down in front of his son and placed his hands on his little shoulders. "Tobias, if your mom were here, she would be so proud of you."

Tobias beamed from ear to ear and returned to skipping down the road. Once his son wasn't looking, Elijah allowed the tears to come.

Jemma

"Are we there yet?" Jemma asked impatiently.

"We've been walking for years," Callum complained.

"It's been eleven days. If you walked faster, it wouldn't take as long," Sparrow said. "Be glad it's still winter. This trip is a lot worse in the heat."

"I'm not sure why they call it winter here," Callum commented. "In Talmar, winter is cold."

"Here in Arydia, it's just slightly less hot," Jemma said.

The path to Illia was long and monotonous. They'd been traveling for over a week, and although they'd seen a few road signs pointing them in the right direction, there was no indication of their distance from the city. They walked past birds and trees and rocks and more birds and trees and rocks. Sparrow said they were lucky that they hadn't been attacked by animals yet, which didn't at all help Jemma sleep at night. She was starting to miss Mistcoast. At least she knew what to expect in that small town.

"Look, Jem!" Callum shouted, pointing at the buildings over the horizon.

Any nostalgia Jemma had felt for Mistcoast disappeared at the sight.

Sparrow, for once, smiled. "Welcome to Illia."

Part 2

The Tide

Jemma

Sparrow paraded the group through the town. Unlike in Mistcoast, no one acknowledged Jemma or commented on the recent trouble she'd caused. They simply ignored her; she was just another face in the crowd, and she loved it.

In an alleyway, Sparrow approached a random door, knocked seven times, paused, then knocked twice more. "Open the door. It's Sparrow."

A small child answered with a grin. "Hi, Sparrow! Oh, you brought friends! Who are you?"

"I'm Jemma, and this is Callum. Who are you?"

"I'm Scraps!" He looked at Sparrow. "Are they allowed inside?"

"Yes. Open the door," Sparrow demanded.

Scraps swung the door open. "Welcome to the thieves' guild!" Inside was a large room with about a dozen people meandering about; they looked unarmed and harmless, but Jemma knew better than to trust their appearances. Cracked wooden tables held games and snacks, and worn-down chairs were scattered about. The right wall held a few ominous doors, each with multiple locks.

"Does the guild have a name?" Callum asked.

"We're workshopping it," a woman said. She reached out a hand. "My name is Zyra."

Callum shook her hand.

Jemma watched the woman carefully. "Is that your real name or your fake name?"

Zyra laughed. "You must be Jemma. Welcome."

Jemma's eyes widened. "How did you know?" Callum asked.

"I know everything," Zyra said. "You must be Callum."

"Is Ash here?" Sparrow asked Zyra.

She shook her head. "He disappeared a few hours ago."

"Where is he?"

Zyra shrugged. "You don't need to know. He'll come back."

Sparrow stormed off into the other room.

Zyra returned her attention to Jemma and Callum. "Is this your first time in Illia?"

The pair nodded.

"Can I show them around?" Scraps asked eagerly.

Jemma looked at Scraps, then moved closer to Zyra to whisper. "Why did you let him into a thieves' guild? He's basically a kid."

Zyra looked her up and down. "The pot calling the kettle black, I see."

Jemma shot her a confused look. What did kitchen equipment have to do with this?

"I'm giving you a tour. Come on!" Scraps pulled at Callum's hand, and Jemma followed behind. They weaved through the tables in the room. "This is where we hang out and play games and eat food," Scraps said before he dragged them to the right wall. "This is where the doors are."

"Where do the doors lead?" Jemma asked.

"Well, that one"—he pointed to the furthest door—"leads to the boss's office. And this one"—he pointed to the closer one—"leads to all the cool guild stuff."

"Like what?" Jemma asked.

"Like money, potions, weapons..."

Jemma grinned. She could probably pick those locks fairly easily. She needed some new daggers.

"I see that look. Don't even think about it," Zyra warned.

Jemma rolled her eyes as Scraps led her to the other side of the room and through a small doorway. Sparrow stood in the middle of the new room, leaning against a counter and drinking from a bottle. "This is the kitchen," Scraps said. "The food in the cabinets is fair game for whoever wants it." Scraps pulled on Callum's hand, dragging him back into the main room and to a small door in the corner. He opened it to show a closet with a mattress on the floor topped by a pillow, a ragged blanket, and a small plush dog. "This is my room!"

"Wait, you live here?" Jemma asked.

"We found him digging for scraps of food in the trash," Zyra said. "Ash figured this was the better alternative."

"Have you ever heard of a treehouse?" Jemma asked Scraps.

"A what?"

"Nevermind." Jemma returned to Zyra's side. "What are we supposed to do here?"

"Wait for Ash to return. He has some sort of mission for you."

Right on cue, a young man burst through the door wearing jeans, a grey t-shirt, and a black leather coat and walked with an air of confidence that forced everyone to jump to conclusions about his personality and motives. With a smirk on his face, he looked over Jemma and Callum. "Welcome, my little spies. Sit down. We need to chat."

Clarissa

Clarissa sat in Abigail's room, watching the girl shaking, coughing. She was still refusing to eat and sleeping only when her body was on the brink of exhaustion. It pained Clarissa to watch, but she couldn't bring herself to leave Abigail all alone. She desperately needed to clean; she hadn't swept the floor or gathered up toys in days, and with ten kids, it took only minutes to make the entire place a mess. She cooked nothing but eggs for breakfast and the same two easy soup recipes on repeat for lunch and dinner. Her inadequacy frustrated her. The kids deserved better than this, and she wanted to be the one to give it to them, but maybe Jareth was right. Maybe the most loving thing she could do for these kids was find them other homes.

Abigail coughed again and rolled over in her bed, accidentally knocking her rabbit onto the floor in the process. "Miss Clarissa, I don't feel good."

"Let me go get your medicine." From the top drawer of a dresser in the corner of the room, Clarissa pulled out the vial and the small measuring cup from Derek. As she poured, the last drop of medicine barely filled the cup.

"Here." She knelt by Abigail's bedside. "Take this. It's the last one, so after this, no more medicine."

"Does that mean I'll feel better then?" Abigail asked.

"Hopefully so," Clarissa said. She couldn't bear to be honest with the girl, yet she couldn't lie to her.

Abigail handed back the measuring cup. She hugged her pillow tight with tears in her eyes. "Am I going to die?"

Clarissa stroked her hair. "No. Of course not." Abigail was going to be okay; Clarissa would make sure of it. She simply needed to take Abigail to Caridelle, to the hospital, and in order to do that, she needed to find homes for the nine other kids that lived in the orphanage.

Her mom had tried and failed in the past to find homes for the kids five years ago when the orphanage first opened. Clarissa wasn't sure if the task was possible, but as Jareth had reminded her, Mistcoast was different than it had been then. It was a city in crisis at the time; people were too busy coping with recent tragedies to take care of the kids most in need. Now, however, things were different. The city had mostly recovered, and people seemed to be doing better. Maybe she could find families to take these kids.

Clarissa shook her head. 'Maybe' wasn't good enough. She *would* find families to take these kids. She had to. She had to take Abigail to Caridelle. It wasn't an option.

She stepped outside of Abigail's bedroom, where a teenager stood alone in the main room. Clarissa hugged her tight.

"Is something wrong?" Eloise asked.

Clarissa pulled away, looking at Eloise with tears in her eyes.

"You're dismantling the orphanage, aren't you?"

"How did you know?"

Eloise shrugged. "Jareth and Derek and I talked about it."

Clarissa sighed. "Do you think I'm making the wrong choice? Am I choosing Abigail over the other kids?"

"No," Eloise said. "You're doing the best thing you can do for them."

"I'm going to need a lot of families to take care of these kids. It's going to be hard to find that many people willing to help."

"The city of Mistcoast loves you, Clarissa," Eloise reminded her. "You'll have all the help you need."

Derek

Gavin tugged on Derek's leg. "Can I come hunting with you today?"

"I want to come too!" Nora said.

"You have school today," Derek argued.

The kids rolled their eyes at him in unison.

Derek chuckled. "Where did you learn to roll your eyes like that?"

Nora pointed at her brother. "Gavin taught me."

Gavin shrugged. "You told me it's good to teach my little sisters," Gavin reminded Derek.

"I meant teaching them reading and math and manners."

Nora grinned at Gavin. "Can you teach me how to fight?"

"No," Derek said. "He doesn't even know how to fight."

"Yes, I do!" Gavin punched at Derek, who caught his fist and grabbed his other hand.

Derek spun Gavin around and held both his wrists. "See, Nora? You don't want to learn to fight from him."

"Can you teach me?" Nora asked Derek eagerly.

Derek shook his head. "No. Go to school, both of you. Where are Kyla and Trevor? You all are going to be late." He glanced around for Tara; she was normally the one to walk with them to school.

"Kyla is skipping sch—" Gavin covered Nora's mouth before she could finish her sentence.

"Kyla isn't here," Gavin said.

"Where's Trevor? Trevor!" Derek yelled the kid's name, and he came running down the stairs. "Alright, I'll take you three to school." He picked up Trevor and placed him on his shoulders.

"I want to ride on your shoulders too!" Nora complained.

"One at a time. You'll get the next turn."

Torin came down the stairs with his bow in his hand. "Are you ready for hunting practice, Derek?"

"I have to take the kids to school first. I'll be right back."

"Isn't that Tara's job? Where is she?" He looked around the house with fury in his eyes.

"Don't worry about it. I'll take them to school."

"You need to practice," Torin argued. "Who cares about school anyways?"

"Not Kyla," Derek mumbled under his breath. He looked at Torin with a sigh. "It'll be quick. I'll be right back." He dragged the kids out the door without giving Torin a chance to argue.

When he returned, Torin was already outside practicing with a target. Derek picked up his bow. He wanted to check on Tara, but he didn't need to incur Torin's wrath today.

"Did the kids make it to school in one piece?"

"All but Kyla," Derek said. "I have no clue where she ran off to."

Torin dropped his bow to his side and turned to look at him. "What do you mean?"

"She skipped school," Derek explained. Although he had avoided his older brother's wrath, he could tell by the look in Torin's eyes that Kyla hadn't. "It's not a big deal," Derek told him. "Tara and I used to skip school all the time at her age."

"And look how you two turned out." Torin shoved a bow into Derek's arms. "You practice. I'm going to find her."

Derek grabbed an arrow out of the quiver on the ground and aimed at the target. He remembered when he and Tara were younger and Torin was out hunting with their dad; it was Derek and Tara's unspoken assignment to keep the younger kids entertained. This was a difficult task in the cramped house, so they often escaped outside into the woods in the opposite direction of wherever Torin and their dad had walked. They played hide-and-seek for hours on end. Derek and Tara often picked easy spots, allowing themselves to get out of the game early and chat while the younger kids played. The game, however, was dangerous to play with kids as stubborn as Derek's siblings. Kyla was competitive and always the last to be found, camouflaging herself with dirt and leaves and hiding high in trees or deep in bushes. Often Torin would arrive home before Kyla had been found, and he would search for her in frustration and annoyance. Only then would Kyla reveal her hiding spot, bragging about the ingenuity of her disguise.

Derek could only hope, for her sake, that Kyla put those hiding skills to good use today.

JARETH

The floors were clean, the shelves were stocked, and the customers were happy. Most importantly, Jareth's mom had remembered the calendar on the wall this morning and was counting down the days until her husband arrived home. Jareth leaned back in his chair and smiled at the clean store before him. Today was a good day.

The front door creaked open, and Clarissa peeked inside. Jareth's smile widened. Today had become an even better day.

"What can I help you with?"

Clarissa leaned against the checkout counter, staring at the wood floor beneath her. "You were right."

"I… what?"

"You were right about the kids. I can't take care of all of them. I know that makes me a failure, but—"

"That doesn't make you a failure. That makes you human."

Clarissa's shoulders relaxed. "Thanks, Jareth." She handed him another grocery list and a pile of coins. "I really hate to ask this of you again, but Tara is watching Abigail, and I need to get back before—"

"Don't worry about it," Jareth said, then frowned. He ran his fingers through his hair. "I'm sorry. I keep interrupting you. I don't mean to—"

"It's okay," Clarissa said with a smile. "I'm going to go talk to some people about the kids and the orphanage. I'll see you later."

"I'll see you later," he echoed as she walked out the door.

He shook his head with a sigh, hoping Clarissa didn't think he was as awkward as he felt.

Clarissa

Clarissa was a helper from a young age. She helped her dad with his carpentry, learning the names of all the tools and handing him each one he called for. She helped her mom cook dinner, chopping ingredients for her mom's recipes and washing the dishes afterwards. She helped the children at the orphanage learn to walk, read, play, and share. She befriended the people of the town too; she helped Mrs. Ellis build a table for her shop, she brought food to Mr. Campbell when his wife passed away, and she visited Mrs. Amans with the kids to cheer her up.

Now, she was the one needing help.

It should have been easy to ask. Everyone loved her. No one would object or be angry or rude. No one would call her selfish or unreasonable for her request. Still, the idea of asking for help left guilt in the pit of her stomach.

She visited Mrs. Ellis's shop first, a small wooden table placed under a small tent for shade. Mrs. Ellis stood with a smile, talking to passersby and trying to sell the bags and wallets she had crafted. She waved as Clarissa approached. "Clarissa, honey, how are you?" she said as she gave Clarissa a hug.

"I'm doing well," Clarissa said. "I have a strange question for you."

"Anything, dear. What is it?"

"So you know I'm in charge of the orphanage now, right?"

"Yes, of course." Mrs. Ellis placed her hand on Clarissa's shoulder. "You're such a sweetheart for looking after those kids."

"Well, the youngest of those kids is very sick. I need to take her to a doctor in Caridelle, and I'm not sure how long we'll be there."

"What about the other kids?"

"That's what I need to talk to you about. I'm looking for people to adopt the other nine kids."

Mrs. Ellis's eyes widened and she took a step back. "Oh. Well… that's what you came here for? That's a big ask, Clarissa. I don't know that I could just agree to that. I mean, I can think about it, and talk to my husband…"

Clarissa nodded. "I understand. I don't expect anyone to make that decision quickly, but would you think about it? You can meet the kids if you'd like. Would you mind also spreading the word? I need to leave for Caridelle as soon as possible."

"I… I'll see what I can do." A customer approached, and Mrs. Ellis's attention was quickly redirected.

She didn't say no. She didn't say yes, but she didn't say no. Maybe the task wouldn't be as impossible as Clarissa had imagined.

She walked back to the orphanage, where Tara and Kyla were waiting for her.

"How was Abigail?" Clarissa asked.

"She slept the whole time," Tara reported. Clarissa wasn't sure whether that was good or bad.

"Can we go to the beach now?" Kyla begged Tara.

Tara nodded. "I promised her a girls' day at the beach," Tara told Clarissa.

Kyla grinned. "*And* we're going to go visit Tara's boyfr—"

Tara clasped a hand over Kyla's mouth halfway through the word.

"Are you skipping school?" Clarissa teased Kyla with a grin.

Tara removed her hand to let Kyla answer the question, and Kyla put a finger over her lips. "Don't tell anyone."

"My lips are sealed," Clarissa promised.

Tara and Kyla left the building, leaving Clarissa alone in silence with a sleeping Abigail. She cleaned the main room by shoving all the toys in the corner and prepped vegetables for soup for dinner. She hated that the toys weren't organized, that the kids' clothes needed to be washed again, that they had run out of eggs five days ago, but she wasn't superhuman. She could only clean and chop vegetables so fast.

Even the most caring people had their limits.

Elijah

"How was school today, kid?" Eli asked.

"It was good! I got to play on the playground with Charlette," Tobias exclaimed.

"Who's Charlette?"

"Cosette's twin sister."

"And who's Cosette?"

"The cute girl in my class!"

Eli teased his hair. "You're too young to be thinking girls are cute." Elijah wasn't near ready to teach him about girls and dating and relationships.

"I don't want to date her, Dad!" Tobias said. "Girls are gross."

"I thought you said they were cute."

"Only Cosette is cute," Tobias clarified.

Tobias laughed as Eli picked him up and placed him on his shoulders. "You can date when you're 50," Eli told his son.

"50? That's so old! You're like 50, Dad!"

"I'm 28!" Eli defended.

"That's still old!" Tobias teased Eli's hair in retaliation.

"Don't mess up my hair; I have to work tonight. I can't look like a total mess." Eli set Tobias down as they entered Cohen's office.

Cohen chuckled. "Hey, kid. Are you staying out of trouble lately?"

Tobias nodded proudly.

"He found a girl at school he thinks is cute," Eli said.

"Girls are more trouble than they're worth," Cohen told the kid. He handed Eli a paper with the description of a job. "One of the rowboats has a little leak. I was hoping you could fix it."

Eli took the paper from him. "I was hoping you had more than one job for me tonight."

"That's all I've got," Cohen said. "Things have been slow around here lately."

"Well, I'll get this done." Eli held up the paper.

"See you tomorrow."

Elijah tugged on his son's hand, pulling him away from the trinkets on Cohen's desk. "Come on, son. I need to finish this job while it's still daylight."

Tobias followed along happily. He sat on the edge of the docks, swinging his feet above the water while his dad worked on the boat. Eli didn't mind the job—it was short and easy, at least—but that also meant it wouldn't pay well. He wiped the sweat off his brow and continued his work, putting on gloves and closing the small hole with sealant.

As he was putting his tools away and removing the gloves, he heard a nearby splash in the water. Immediately, he guessed the cause of the noise. He dove into the water after his son, hugging him tight with one arm and holding onto the dock with the other.

"Dad, I'm okay! I know how to swim!" Tobias assured his dad as he climbed back onto the dock.

"Were you trying to go for a swim, or did you fall?" Eli asked.

"I was trying to drink the water."

Elijah laughed. "Seawater doesn't taste good, kid."

"But I was thirsty!"

Elijah packed up his tools and took Tobias's hand. "Let's go home and get something better to drink."

"Apple juice?"

"Water. We don't have apple juice."

"What about orange juice?"

"We have water, and we have sandwiches, and there might be one more orange in the kitchen."

Tobias sighed in an overdramatized show of emotion. "That'll work."

Elijah returned the paper, now soaked in salt water, to Cohen and led his son towards their house. It was a small home consisting of a single room, with two beds, a table, and wooden boxes that acted as kitchen counters. Eli had built most of the furniture himself. It wasn't perfect or polished, but it was functional, and to Eli and Tobias, that was all that mattered.

Elijah opened one of the wooden boxes and dug around for fruit. "I was wrong, Tobias. We don't have any oranges."

"Do we have sandwiches?"

Elijah broke open a piece of bread and shoved two thin slices of fish inside from his catch that morning. He poured water from a pitcher into a small cup and handed it to Tobias along with the sandwich. "Here, kid."

Tobias smiled. "I love you, Dad."

Elijah sat down beside him. "I love you too."

"Aren't you hungry?"

Elijah shook his head.

"You're never hungry, Dad."

"You'll understand when you're older."

"I'm older now! I'm eight!"

Elijah hugged his son. "You're growing too fast. We're going to have to shrink you back down."

"No, I'm getting taller! I'm almost as tall as Cosette!"

Elijah rolled his eyes. "You're too young to date."

Tobias giggled. "You're too old to date."

"I'm not old!" Elijah said, gently tackling his son. Tobias laughed and fought back, to no avail. Elijah pinned him down. "See? When I'm old, I won't be able to do this anymore."

"When you're old, I can tackle you instead."

Eli chuckled. "You've got a long time until then, kid."

Jareth

Jareth walked down the road towards the orphanage. He saw the kids playing outside on the playground centered between their home and the neighboring school, supervised by a tired Eloise. She waved at him as he passed. "Clarissa is inside."

He opened the door of the orphanage and headed towards the kitchen. If Clarissa had seen him enter, she would have offered, nearly insisted, on putting the groceries away herself, but she was nowhere to be found, presumably in Abigail's room. In the kitchen, Jareth found Owen stuffing blueberries in his mouth. Jareth sighed.

"Owen, what are you doing?"

"I was hungry!"

"That doesn't mean you get to steal food out of the kitchen."

"It's fruit! It's healthy!"

"It's *expensive* fruit. We're almost out of those at the store." Jareth handed him an apple and took the box of blueberries from him.

"How are you almost out? Who's eating all the blueberries?"

"You are." Jareth unpacked the fabric bags of food into the cabinets. He'd seen Clarissa organize the groceries enough lately to know where everything belonged.

"Why are you here all the time? Why does that other guy come? Why is Miss Clarissa always in Abigail's room?"

"Abigail's sick. Clarissa is trying to take care of her. Why don't you go play outside?"

"I'm tired of playing outside."

"Go outside with Eloise and the others."

Owen glared at him. "You're not the boss of me."

Jareth sighed. The kid wasn't wrong. "Okay, but don't steal any more blueberries." He set the empty bags on the counter and headed to find Clarissa. The door creaked as he peeked it open.

Clarissa sat on the floor, holding a sleeping Abigail. She brought a finger to her lips, silently begging Jareth to be quiet. Slowly and gently, she placed Abigail in her bed and stepped out of the room. "Hey, Jareth."

"I left the groceries in the kitchen. Owen was in there eating blueberries."

Clarissa sighed. "I don't know what to do about him." Jareth followed her to the kitchen, where Owen had reopened the box of blueberries.

"Go play outside with Eloise," she said.

"I don't want to play with Eloise," Owen said. "I want to play with you."

"I have to sit with Abigail," Clarissa said. She kept glancing back at Abigail's room with worry, as if the girl would become more sick only when she wasn't being observed.

"I can go play with you outside," Jareth suggested.

Owen tilted his head, considering the offer. "Do I get a piggyback ride?" he countered.

Jareth knelt down, and Owen climbed on his back.

"You don't have to do this," Clarissa told him.

"I don't mind," Jareth said as he carried Owen out of the room. The kid rode happily on his back as they walked out of the orphanage and around to the side of the building.

"But the playground is that way!" Owen pointed behind them.

“I have to do something first.” Jareth walked to the donation box on the side of the building and dumped in a red bag of coins.

Owen gasped. “Where did you get all that money?”

“It’s a long story,” Jareth said. It wasn’t a story that a seven-year-old would understand. They headed towards the playground.

“Are you rich, Jareth?” Owen asked.

Jareth chuckled. “No one in this town is rich, Owen.”

“Well, I’m going to be rich when I grow up.”

Jareth grinned. “I wish the world were as simple as you believe.”

Derek

Derek and Torin returned home after a long afternoon of archery practice and a bit of failed hunting. Derek had spent half the day by himself practicing while Torin searched for their elusive sisters. Thankfully, he hadn't found them.

As Derek approached their home, he heard laughter from two girls inside. He recognized the voices immediately. Unfortunately, so did Torin, who stormed towards the house and slammed the door open.

"Where have you been all day?" he immediately demanded of Kyla.

"I was with Tara!" Kyla defended.

Torin's glare moved to Tara. "You let her skip school?"

"I took her to the beach for a day. Calm down."

Derek tried to move past Torin, determined to stand closer to Tara than his brother did, but Torin stood in the doorway to the house, an immovable object directly in Derek's desired path. As much as he wanted to be, Derek wasn't an unstoppable force.

"You helped her skip school," Torin accused.

"I helped her relax," Tara countered. "Mom didn't care."

"Mom knew about this?"

"Mom watched Alec for me."

"Kyla, go to your room," Derek yelled. Torin took a step towards Tara, and Derek took the chance to push his way into the house. He stood between his siblings, facing Torin.

"Why can't I talk to my sister?" Torin asked.

"Are you going to hit her?" Derek said.

"I haven't decided yet."

Derek threw the first punch, and Torin didn't hesitate to fight back. "Boys, stop it," Tara demanded, but her brothers didn't listen. Derek took a few punches before Torin, satisfied with the pain he had caused, backed off and stormed out of the house.

"You held back," Tara said quietly.

Derek nodded. "I don't want to hurt him."

Tara placed a hand on his shoulder. "Then why would you fight him?"

"To keep him from fighting you."

Tara shook her head. "You don't have to protect me. Torin is dumb, but he won't kill me. My life isn't on the line."

Derek pushed Tara's hand off his shoulder. "I need to go check on Kyla."

Tara grabbed his arm before he could leave. "Your face is covered in blood. I'll do it."

After Tara walked away, Derek sat on the couch. Tara was wrong. He needed to protect her. Torin was reckless and angry. He wouldn't hesitate to hurt her, and Derek simply couldn't allow that.

He had to find a better way to protect his sister from her own optimism.

Jemma

"So they want you to infiltrate the Red Coin?" Sparrow asked.

"Infiltrate," Callum said with a grin. "That's such a cool spy word."

"Why don't I get to infiltrate the Red Coin?" Sparrow questioned. She sat across from them at the kitchen table of Ash's home. He had given them a key and offered to let them stay there for the night before disappearing.

"Ash said they might recognize you," Jemma told Sparrow. "We've never been to Illia. We can lie and say we're new Red Coin members."

"Don't get caught," Sparrow warned.

"We're professionals," Jemma reminded her with a grin.

Her brow raised. "Really? Everyone in Mistcoast knows who you are. You've never had to fake an identity."

"I'm sure we can handle it," Jemma said.

"And Ash said we can use fake names!" Callum argued. "I'm going to be Storm. She's going to be Sky."

"Did Ash approve these names?" Sparrow asked.

"Yes!"

"Really?"

"Well... his exact words were 'they sound like the kind of stupid names Red Coin members would come up with.'"

"Right. Did he tell you anything about the Red Coin?"

"He told us that he hates them."

Sparrow leaned back in her chair. "What else did he tell you?"

"He wants us to figure out who the guild leader is and a bunch of other secrets," Jemma said, "but apparently we have to make friends first before we ask too many questions." She held up a piece of folded parchment. "We're also supposed to deliver this message to some guy named Keiran."

"What does it say?"

"We didn't read it," Callum told Jemma. "Ash said not to."

"Good," Sparrow said as she stood from the table. "Go to sleep."

"Where are you going?" Jemma asked as Sparrow walked towards the door.

"Out," Sparrow answered as the door shut behind her.

"She's right; we should sleep. I call the couch," Callum said.

"Why would you call the couch when it's a two-bedroom apartment?"

"Ash isn't going to let us sleep in his room."

"Right. You could have called the other bed."

Callum grabbed a blanket and spread it over the couch. "Have you ever thought, Jemma, that maybe I'm trying to be nice?"

She realized she hadn't. She'd never really assumed anyone to be 'nice'. "Whatever. Goodnight." Jemma walked off to the spare bedroom and curled up under the thin blanket. 'Nice' wasn't really in her vocabulary. She spent too much time around people and saw too many of their flaws to think about positive descriptors like that. If anyone in the world was 'nice', however, it was most definitely Callum.

Elijah

"Dad, can I go fishing with you today?"

Elijah sighed as he tossed his lunch into his bag. "You have school."

"But I don't want to go to school! I don't *want* to!"

"Remember, sometimes we have to do—"

"—things we don't want to do." Tobias finished the saying with clear annoyance in his tone. It was a quote Tobias's mom had learned from a friend and repeated over and over again when Tobias was a tantrum-throwing toddler. Elijah had continued the saying long after she was gone.

"Grab your backpack. Let's go." Elijah held his son's hand as they walked out the door and towards the school.

Tobias dragged his feet through the dirt. "I don't want to."

As they neared the school, Tobias walked slower and slower, moving his feet as little as possible with every step. Elijah stopped walking. "Tobias. You have to go to school. It's not optional."

Tobias shook his head. "I don't like it."

"But you liked it yesterday! You got to play on the playground with friends. And there was that cute girl, remember?" He didn't want to encourage this 'cute girl' thing, but if it got Tobias to go to school willingly, maybe the pros outweighed the cons.

"Can I just skip school today? Just one day?" Tears ran down his cheeks as he begged his dad.

Elijah paused walking and knelt down to Tobias's level. "Tobias, seriously, why are you acting like this?"

"We're making paper flowers at school today."

Elijah looked at his son with genuine confusion. "Paper flowers? That sounds fun," he lied. It didn't sound fun, but it didn't sound like something to have a breakdown over.

"It's not fun!" Tobias yelled. He stared at the ground, and his voice became a barely audible mumble. "It's just... sad."

"Sad? Why are paper flowers sad?"

"They're for the spring festival."

Well that explained it. Elijah sighed. Yes, it was a national holiday, but why did the teachers feel the need to remind the kids of their trauma? Although maybe he should give them the benefit of the doubt. Maybe most of the kids in his class were too young to remember the history of this town. Tobias, however, remembered well, and although he hardly dwelled on it, he didn't need to spend an entire school day being reminded.

Eli picked up his crying son. "Do you know what I do when I'm sad?"

"What?"

"I go fishing," he answered as he carried his son towards the docks.

Jareth

Jareth closed up the shop at the end of the day with Mr. Campbell breathing down his neck. He had planned on closing earlier since business had been slow for the afternoon, but when his boss showed up, he knew that was no longer an option. Mr. Campbell watched closely as Jareth swept the floor and counted the coins in the drawer, as if Jareth hadn't been successfully performing the same repetitive job for almost a year now. Once the shop was perfectly clean and Mr. Campbell approved, he left for home.

"How was work today?" his mom asked as he entered the house.

"Good."

"How is Clarissa? Did she come by today?"

"She came by yesterday," Jareth said as he searched the kitchen cabinets for a snack.

"How are the kiddos doing?"

"Well, little Abigail is a little sick."

"Oh..." His mom stared at the ground. "Will she be alright?"

"I'm sure she will be." Jareth found some bread and smeared strawberry jam on it. The bread was questionably stale, but it probably wouldn't kill him. With his snack in one hand and his book in the other, he headed towards the door.

"Where are you going?" his mom asked.

"To meet up with a friend."

"Okay. Bye, Jareth! Have fun!"

He ate the snack as he walked towards the docks, the sound of crashing waves growing louder as he neared them. He entered Reece's tavern quietly, pushing through the talkative crowds to reach the bar in the back where he sat down and opened his spell book.

Reece slid him a drink.

"No thanks," Jareth said without looking up from his book.

"It's just water."

"I'm not thirsty."

"Good." Reece picked back up the cup and splashed the water at him.

Instinctively, Jareth cast a shield spell—not around himself, but around the spell book, protecting the fragile pages of the rare tome. He tensed as the cold water hit him in the face.

"You could have protected yourself and the book," Reece pointed out.

"You didn't give me much time to think about it. Don't damage my book."

"I would have fixed it with magic." Reece tossed Jareth a towel. "Besides, I wanted to see how quick your reaction time and casting time are getting. That was pretty impressive," he said with a grin.

"Why are you so insistent that I master the shield spell?"

"It's one of the most useful spells in combat. It might save your life one day, or someone else's. You could be a hero," Reece said as he dried the cup.

"This isn't Talmar. People don't just attack in the streets."

Reece froze. "Did you forget about—"

"Of course not, but that was a one-time event. I'm not going to be fighting anyone anytime soon."

Reece shrugged. "You never know what adventure lies ahead."

Derek

Derek punched his opponent in the nose with three quick jabs. The guy staggered back but recovered quicker than Derek expected and struck him in the gut, knocking the air out of him.

"Come on, Derek," Tara yelled from the crowd. Her shouted words always sounded judgemental, but Derek took them as encouragement.

It reminded him what he was fighting for: for Tara, for Kyla, for all his siblings who desperately needed him and the money from winning.

He punched again, and again, and again, and got punched again, and again, and again. This guy wouldn't let him win easily, but Derek did eventually win. He stepped out of the ring, bruised and beaten, and went to claim his prize money.

Tara followed behind him. "How much did this one pay?"

"Enough to get food for a week," Derek said as he approached the man in charge, a guy named Kane who looked like he could beat up anyone in the room but never actually entered a fight.

"Nice job," Kane said as he handed Derek a pouch of coins. "We had someone cancel for Saturday; they had to go to a wedding or something stupid. Do you want another fight?"

"Who's it against?"

"Noah."

"Sure," Derek agreed. That would be an easy win.

"Great. See you then."

"Hey, Kane," Tara peeked out from behind Derek and waved with a smile.

Kane—who Derek had never seen grin at anything but the sight of blood and money—smiled back. "Hey, Tara. Are you coming on Saturday?"

"If Derek's fighting, I'll be here."

Derek shook his head. "I didn't say you could come—"

Kane interrupted him. "I should schedule Derek to fight more often then."

"Alright, we're leaving," Derek said as he pulled Tara away.

"Bye, Kane!"

"Goodbye, Tara."

Derek rolled his eyes, but held back his opinions until they were outside the building. "Since when are you flirting with him? Out of all people, Tara..."

"Remember when you asked me to go get your money so you could run off with Clarissa? Well, I asked around, and they said Kane had the money, so I went to get it, and we started talking, and..."

Derek cursed under his breath. This was his own fault.

"He's a pretty cool guy," Tara said.

"He could kill you if he wanted to," Derek reminded her.

"So could you," she said, "yet you choose not to."

"You're my sister."

"Exactly. I've had 18 years to drive you insane. I've given you plenty of reasons to kill me."

Derek laughed. "You have such a weird sense of humor."

Tara shrugged. "I learned it from my older brother."

"From Torin?" Derek joked.

Tara rolled her eyes. "Have you ever seen Torin laugh?"

"I think Alec will learn to laugh before Torin does."

Tara slowed her walk and gazed up at the stars, lost deep in her thoughts for a moment before she looked back at Derek with her usual teasing grin. "We should play a game. If I can make Torin laugh before you do, you owe me a house."

"A house?"

"A house, so I can move out."

"You wouldn't survive without me," Derek teased.

"Hey, I moved out once before, and I'm still alive."

"You lived in a basement for a month."

"It had a couch!" Tara defended. "But fine. You can come live in my imaginary house with me so I don't die."

"The house that you think I'm going to buy you?"

Tara nodded.

Derek shook his head and chuckled. "Wow, that's so generous of you."

"You're welcome," Tara said with a smirk. She skipped along the path down the dark road as they headed home for the night.

Jemma

Callum and Jemma entered the Red Coin hideout through an inconspicuous door in an empty, dark alley. The area of Illia they traversed to arrive here had been dead—the "normal" citizens had already gone to sleep—but the Red Coin was wide awake. Music blared through the building, almost drowning out the words of the guys who greeted them as they entered.

"Do you two know where you are?" a blond teenager asked. He leaned against the wall and propped his hand on the hilt of his sheathed sword.

Jemma rolled her eyes. "Do you know where you are?"

"Answer the question," the other teenager demanded. He stood in the middle of the hallway, blocking Jemma and Callum from entering further. Despite his attempt to look intimidating, he didn't scare Jemma. She was much more worried about the boy leaning against the wall who seemed so confidently unbothered by their presence.

Callum fished a small necklace out from under his shirt, showing a pendant with an intricate symbol engraved in silver.

The blond boy grabbed the pendant and pulled it right up to his face to study it closely, jerking Callum's neck forward in the process. "Looks legit," he told the other kid before turning back to Jemma and Callum. "You must be new around here."

"New to Illia, not new to the guild. We came from Caridelle."

The blond boy chuckled. "Oh, so you're rich kids."

"Only because we steal from the rich kids."

"Well, there's less opportunity for that in Illia. Maybe you should have stayed in Caridelle." The blond boy pointed to his friend. "That's Finn. I'm Kai."

"Don't cause any trouble here," Finn warned.

"Relax, Finn. They're friends. What are your names?"

Callum pointed to Jemma. "That's Sky. I'm Storm."

"Is there a band back there? They sound good." Jemma wandered a few steps down the hallway, but Finn stood in her way.

"Whoa, hold up. You can't just walk in here like that."

"But I'm one of you," Jemma said.

"Maybe that's how things work in Caridelle, but not here. I'll let Ember know we have some newbies. She'll want to meet you and ask some questions before she lets you in. Come back tomorrow."

"But we want to party," Jemma said.

"Then go home and party," Kai said. "Trust me, I wish I could let you in, but Finn's right. That's not how this works."

"But—"

"We'll come back tomorrow," Callum said. He walked outside, leaving Jemma no choice but to follow.

"What are you doing?" Jemma asked in a hushed, frustrated voice as soon as they were out of earshot of Kai and Finn.

"There's another door into this place," Callum reminded her.

Jemma sighed. "Right. You're right."

"Ash mentioned one on the west side."

Jemma looked around. "Which way is west?"

After a bit of wandering and an instance of accidental breaking-and-entering, they finally found the correct door. This one led to a much larger and busier foyer. People meandered about with drinks in their hands, and a few waved at Jemma and Callum as they entered.

"Why aren't these people stopping us like the other guys?" Callum whispered.

Jemma shrugged. "I think they're too drunk to care."

A few people stepped through a large door across the foyer, giving Jemma and Callum a peek into the adjacent room. It was crowded and dark, lit only by magical floating lights, and seemed to be the source of the live music they heard earlier.

"Come on! Let's go there!" Callum begged. "We can talk to people. We can make friends."

"Right. We have to make friends," Jemma mumbled with a tinge of annoyance, but she let Callum drag her through the door into the crowd.

Music played by a small band on a corner stage blared through the room. Small glowing orbs floated in the rafters. People were packed tighter than fish caught in a net. By the time Jemma had surveyed the room, deciding who she could take in a fight and who to avoid, Callum had already struck up a conversation.

"Sky! Meet my new friend, Luna. Luna, this is my best friend, Sky."

Luna smiled at Jemma. She brushed her long blonde hair from her face and shook Jemma's hand. "Nice to meet you, Sky. Storm said you just moved here from Caridelle."

"Yeah, that's right," Jemma said.

"Have you scheduled a meeting yet with Ethan or Ember?"

"We met Ember yesterday," Jemma said. "Is she the one in charge around here? Or is that Ethan? Or is it someone else?"

"There's a complex chain of command," Luna explained, "but Ember's at the top of it."

Jemma looked around the room to hide her grin from Luna. This was the number one piece of information Ash had requested, and she had gotten it easily. Being a spy wasn't too hard after all.

"So, for what reason did you leave Caridelle?" Luna asked. "It's a beautiful city. I travelled with my father there on business trips when I was younger."

"Um... well... Caridelle..." Callum stumbled over his words before Jemma intervened.

"It's a long story," Jemma said. "We accidentally crossed the wrong people."

"Is Ember aware?"

Jemma nodded. "She knows, unfortunately."

"That's for the best. Ember despises secrets." Luna waved to someone across the room. "Sky, Storm, come with me. I'll introduce you to my friends."

Jemma grinned and followed her newfound acquaintance.

Clarissa

Clarissa grabbed Owen's arm before he could run off. "Owen, you have to go to school. You have to put on a shirt."

"I don't want to wear that shirt!"

"It's the only clean shirt you have, Owen." Clarissa sighed in frustration. She would have washed clothes yesterday if she had known this shirt would cause such a fuss.

Clarissa felt a tap on her shoulder, and Sara whispered in her ear. "Melody is in our room crying, and she won't talk to me."

"Okay, I'll try to figure out what's going on." Clarissa tossed Owen's shirt on the floor, momentarily forfeiting one battle for another, but as she took two steps towards Sara's room, Eloise blocked her path. "Mrs. Ellis is at the door."

"Go check on Melody if you get a chance. But get yourself ready for school first! I want you there on time. I'll bring Melody late if I need to." It was Eloise's second-to-last week of secondary school, and Clarissa didn't want her missing a single day.

She set aside the kids' morning routine and walked to the front of the orphanage. She took a deep breath, tuned out the chaos behind her, put on a smile that didn't reach her eyes, and answered the door. "Good morning, Mrs. Ellis."

The woman responded with a soft smile back. "Hi, Clarissa. I wanted to let you know that I talked with my husband last night. We had a long conversation about it, and we decided we can take in two of the kids—"

Clarissa hugged her immediately. "Thank you. Thank you so much."

"I'm sorry that we only have two extra beds."

"Don't apologize. I can't thank you enough," Clarissa responded. "Have you met Cosette and Charlette? I think they're going to love you."

"Can I meet them now?" Mrs. Ellis asked.

Clarissa glanced back inside the orphanage just in time to see Owen throw his shirt at Sara's face. "It's going to be a busy morning. Maybe come back after school."

Mrs. Ellis nodded in understanding. "I'll be at the market for the day, but I'll come back after I close shop."

"Do you mind waiting here for just a second?" Clarissa asked. Mrs. Ellis nodded, and Clarissa rushed into the kitchen to scribble down a grocery list. Her handwriting was getting progressively worse; she desperately hoped Jareth could still read it. She handed the paper and a pouch of coins to Mrs. Ellis. "Could you give this to Jareth for me?"

"Of course, dear," Mrs. Ellis said.

"Thank you. I'll see you this afternoon." After one more hug, Clarissa closed the door with a sigh of relief. Mrs. Ellis would adopt the twins, and Clarissa wouldn't have to separate them. She only needed to find homes for six more kids (since Eloise was graduating soon), and she had already talked to multiple families who might be willing. Then, once all was settled, she would take Abigail to Caridelle, to a doctor who could diagnose her illness and provide a cure. Abigail would recover, and the other kids wouldn't be hurt in the process.

In the meantime, Clarissa needed to figure out how to tell the kids that they were moving to new homes.

Jareth

Jareth shoved his magic book in his bag in preparation for his daily meeting with Reece and rummaged through the kitchen to find lunch to take to work. His mom sat at the table, playing her usual repetitive card game.

"Jareth, can you grab some carrots on the way home from school? I'm thinking about making a stew for dinner."

Jareth paused. "After school?"

His mom nodded. "Right. Go to school first. Your father won't be very happy if you skip school. Speaking of your father, have you seen him this morning? He wasn't home when I woke up."

Jareth carefully stepped towards his mother, as if the slightest noise or sudden movement could break her, and gently sat down at the table across from her. "Where do you think Dad is?"

"I'm not sure, Jareth. That's why I asked you. I assume he's out running a quick errand. He wouldn't have gone to work without telling me good morning first."

"Right, of course," Jareth said calmly. He wasn't sure what to do. Her memory had been fading, but this part was new. It was as if she travelled through time to a day from years ago. Jareth debated the options in his head. Should he argue with her perceived reality? Would that progress to anything beneficial? Should he allow her to live in delusion? Was telling her that her memory was failing kind or cruel?

"I'll get carrots on the way home from school," he promised. He stood up from the table and took a muffin out of the cabinet. He wasn't sure that counted as lunch, but he wasn't sure he cared. As he stashed the muffin in his bag, he looked at the book. His training with Reece would have to wait; he didn't want to leave his mom alone at home any longer than he had to. Abandoning his mom for work was already scary enough. He couldn't risk leaving her even longer. He slowly drew the spell book from the bag and placed it back on its shelf.

He hugged his mom before heading out the door. "Bye, Mom. I love you."

"I love you too, honey! Make good grades and good friends."

Jareth smiled. "I will."

His smile disappeared the moment he stepped out the door. He wasn't good at faking the emotion, and if his mom was as perceptive as she had been a few years ago, she would have seen right through him.

The walk to work felt longer than normal. Despite the abandoned weight of the spell book, his backpack felt heavier, weighing on his shoulders like a burden he was barely strong enough to carry. His dad would come home in just over a week, eight days, less than the fingers he had on his hands. It felt so close, yet so far away. He tried to care for his mother, and he wanted to believe that he had done well in his father's stead, but the best thing for her was for him to come home. He hated counting down the days until his father returned. He wanted to be independent, to take care of his mother on his own, to handle the responsibilities like the grown adult that he was.

He walked into the grocery store. Dark and dreary clouds blocked the sunlight that typically beamed through the windows. He set down his bag and waited for the customers to enter.

The day was boring and slow, as was typical on days full of clouds and sprinkled rain. A few apathetic customers came and went before Mrs. Ellis entered with a smile. "Good morning, Jareth."

Jareth smiled back. "How is your shop going?"

"It's a slow day," Mrs. Ellis said. She handed Jareth a small piece of paper and a bag of coins. "This is from Clarissa. Would you mind bringing her groceries when you get off of work?"

He looked down at the list. It was full of the normal requests: ingredients for stews, soups, and sandwiches, and plenty of fruit. He normally brought her groceries without question, but... well, it shouldn't take long, and surely his mom couldn't get herself into too much trouble. She rarely even left the house.

Jareth shoved the list into his pocket. "I can bring her groceries. It's no problem."

"You're a good kid, Jareth."

He shrugged. "I try my best."

After work, he packed up the groceries for Clarissa and headed towards the orphanage. The kids were sitting down at the table, eating some fish and bread.

"Where'd you get fish?" Jareth asked Clarissa.

"I bought it from Elijah," she said as she took the bags of groceries from him.

"Have you told the kids yet?"

"Told us what?" one of the girls asked.

"Nothing, Sara. Don't worry about it."

"But now I want to know."

Clarissa looked at Jareth and sighed. "I guess now is as good of a time as ever. Can you..." She glanced back at the closed bedroom door. "Can you watch Abigail for a bit? She's awake and strangely talkative today. I'm hoping that's a good sign, but I think she may just be getting restless from staying in her room for so many days."

"I'll watch her," Jareth agreed. He stepped into Abigail's room, quietly closing the door behind him.

"Who are you?" Abigail asked.

"A friend of Clarissa's," Jareth said.

"Are you her boyfriend?"

Jareth shook his head. "No, I'm just a friend."

"Is that guy with the medicine her boyfriend?"

He assumed she meant Derek. "I don't think so." He secretly hoped not.

"Can I get a boyfriend?" Abigail asked.

"How old are you?"

"I'm six."

"I think you'll have to wait a few more years then."

They heard one of the kids yelling at Clarissa outside the door. "What's going on out there?" Abigail asked. She slowly pushed her blanket aside, clutched her toy rabbit close to her chest as if it would protect her, and stumbled towards the door.

"Don't worry about it. Lay back down." Jareth stood in her path.

"Is someone in trouble?"

"Everything is fine. Don't worry about it."

She slowly went back to her bed and hid under the blanket. "I don't like it when they yell," she said, her voice muffled by the fabric.

Jareth sighed. "Me neither, Abigail."

Clarissa

"So you're leaving us?"

Clarissa sighed. "Sara, that's not what I said."

"You can't leave!" Charlette screamed.

"I'm not leaving you! I'm finding a better place for you to stay. With an actual family."

"This is my family!" Sara argued.

"I need to take Abigail to Caridelle, and—"

"So you care about Abigail more than us," Isaac accused with crossed arms.

"Isaac, you're twelve," Eloise said. "You don't know what you're talking about. You don't understand yet."

"Are you saying I'm stupid?" Isaac yelled.

Eloise shook her head calmly. "No, I'm saying you're immature."

"What if you make us go stay somewhere else and we hate it?" Cosette asked.

"Then I'll figure something else out," Clarissa promised. "I'm not ditching you. I'm trying to do what's best for you."

"Why do you get to decide what's best for us?" Sara asked.

"Because it's my job!" Clarissa said. "It's my responsibility to decide what's best for you, whether you like it or not. That's how parenting works."

"You're a horrible parent," Tristan said. "Don't make us leave. I don't want to leave."

"I'm not making you leave. I'm just... I'm finding a better place for you to stay."

"That sounds like the same thing," Isaac said.

"Well, I'm not leaving!" Owen said, throwing his plate on the ground in anger. It shattered loudly, and food splattered on the wooden floor.

"You don't even like it here," Charlette reminded him.

"You complain all the time too," Sara told Charlette.

"No, I don't! You—"

Amidst the arguing children, Clarissa heard a knock at the door. It took her a second to remember that Mrs. Ellis was coming by to meet the twins.

"Eloise, can you take the kids to the playground?" Clarissa asked.

"You're kicking us out already?" Tristan yelled.

"No, I'm letting you play outside like you're always begging to. Charlette and Cosette, stay here. Everyone else, follow Eloise."

After plenty of groaning and mumbling and an argument to get Owen to put his shoes on, they finally headed outside past Mrs. Ellis towards the playground. Clarissa sighed and smiled at Mrs. Ellis. "Come inside. I want to introduce you to Charlette and Cosette."

The girls waved awkwardly, but Mrs. Ellis managed the tension like a professional. Clarissa watched as the twins slowly relaxed. Soon, they were laughing together, talking about their new home. They didn't seem overly excited, and the nervousness hadn't entirely gone away, but they seemed calm and comfortable. Most importantly, they would have the love and care and attention that Clarissa struggled to provide. She watched the girls with a bittersweet smile, a genuine joy mixed with a bit of remorse and a touch of jealousy that she would never admit.

She stepped into Abigail's room. "Thanks for watching her." She followed Jareth to the front door and opened it for him. "Did Abigail seem okay?"

Jareth laughed. "She kept asking me questions about dating."

Clarissa rolled her eyes with a grin. "I'm sorry about that."

"Don't apologize. I was the one who made the mistake of mentioning I'd never been on a date, and she felt the need to give me lots of advice."

"Was it good advice?"

Jareth shrugged. "It wasn't horrible."

"Well, if you ever take her advice, let me know how it goes."

"I will." Jareth waved as he walked off, and Clarissa closed the door behind him. She stepped back from the door and watched him walk away through the window before catching herself in the act. Although he was in the middle of a public space, it felt intrusive to observe him like that.

As she turned to look away, she noticed him take a step towards the orphanage building, pull out a bag of coins—the same one she had sent to pay for groceries—and dump it in the donation box. She rushed outside. "Jareth! I saw that!"

With a smug grin on his face, he shoved his hands in his jacket pockets and walked away.

Elijah

"Good evening," Elijah said as he sat across from Cohen at his desk.

Cohen sighed and avoided eye contact, which told Elijah all he needed to know.

"You don't have any jobs for me today."

Cohen shook his head. "I don't. I'm sorry."

"I dropped Tobias off at my sister's house so I could get more jobs done today without the kid slowing me down."

"Business is unpredictable. You know this. Sometimes we get a bunch of damaged boats in a week, and other times we don't. It depends on the weather, the pirates, the trade patterns..."

Eli leaned forward in his chair. "And let me guess—I still owe you my boat payment for this week."

"Yes, but that's not my decision. My boss is really the one you owe that money to. If it were up to me, I would have forgotten that debt a year ago."

Eli tossed Cohen a few coins as he stood up. "There's half of it. That's all I have, and I'm lucky to have that much."

"Where'd you get it?"

"I caught quite a bit today. Sold it all to Clarissa."

"She overpaid you."

"She insisted on it." Elijah shook his head. "I think she knew I needed it."

"How?" Cohen asked.

Eli sighed. "That girl knows everything. Look, I'll try to get you the other half of the payment as soon as I can. But I have to feed my kid. That comes first, no matter how mad your boss gets about it."

Elijah walked out of the office and returned to his sister's house. She answered the door with a concerned look on her face. "You're back soon."

"I know. Where's Tobias?"

Sophia stepped aside and let Elijah into the house.

Tobias was peering over the edge of a table at a weapon that Eli instantly recognized. "Look, Dad!" Tobias shouted. "A sword!"

"Where'd you get that?" Eli asked his sister.

"I took it from the house when Dad died."

Elijah carefully picked up his father's sword and unsheathed the blade. It felt wrong, like holding something stolen, something forbidden. The sword held stories told at family gatherings and around campfires, legends of adventures from his father's younger days of fighting dragons and completing epic quests.

"Do you know how to use a sword, Dad?" Tobias asked.

"No, I don't, kid."

"You could always learn," Tobias said.

Eli chuckled. "I don't think so. I kill fish, not wolves and bears and dragons." He swung the sword through the air a few times.

"You should keep it," Sophia said.

Elijah shook his head. "I couldn't take it from you. It's an important part of Dad's legacy."

"Which is why you should have it," Sophia argued. "Pass it on to Toby when he's older."

"I get a sword!" Tobias shouted excitedly.

"One day. Not today." Elijah carefully slid the sword back into its sheath. "Thanks, Sophia."

Sophia smiled back. "Of course."

With a sword in one hand and Tobias's small hand in the other, Elijah headed back home with stories of his father's adventures playing in his mind.

Jemma

Jemma skipped along the road as she wandered back to Ash's apartment. She and Callum had made it their mission for the day to explore Illia and learn the layout of the town. After dinner, they ran into Luna and stayed up much later than necessary hanging out at her house, although Callum (or "Storm", as Luna called him) got tired and went home much earlier than Jemma. Jemma wanted to stay as long as possible, to become close friends with Luna. They talked about Luna's crush, about Jemma's treehouse, about the best types of daggers to throw at trees, but most importantly, they talked about the Red Coin. Jemma learned a lot about their leadership and processes, information that she hoped Ash would find valuable. She even learned about an upcoming party that Kieran would be attending—the perfect time to slip him the note from Ash. She wanted nothing more than to make him proud.

After a few wrong turns in the dark of night, she finally arrived back at Ash's house. The front door, to her surprise, was left ajar. She pulled out two daggers, one for each hand—despite the fact that she hadn't learned dual-wielding yet—and pushed the door open further.

The room was pitch black, and she heard a muffled noise that seemed to come from the bedroom ahead. She wandered forward, stumbling on something in the middle of the floor and immediately readying herself for a fight, but no one came at her. She continued into the bedroom where she saw a cowering, candlelit figure, his face wet with tears. "Callum?"

"Jem?"

"What's wrong?" she asked from a distance.

"They followed me," he said. "Those boys from the Red Coin."

"What did they steal?"

"Um... I don't know. Just some gold, I think."

Jemma sighed. "Ash is going to kill us."

"He... he can't."

Jemma gave a puzzled look that Callum couldn't see. "What do you mean?"

"He's gone."

"Where did he go?"

"You don't get it, Jem!" Callum yelled, his voice shaking in panicked terror. He took a deep breath. "He's dead, Jemma. He's dead on the living room floor."

Part 3

The Waves

Jemma

"You're telling me Callum led the Red Coin straight to Ash?" Zyra asked.

"Not intentionally!" Jemma argued.

Zyra loaded her crossbow. "Where is that boy?"

"I don't know."

Zyra grabbed Jemma's arm. "You know where he is."

"You're going to hurt him."

Zyra nodded. "You're right."

Sparrow leaned against the wall, picking dirt out from under her fingernails. "There are consequences to his actions."

"I can't tell you where he is. I can't let you hurt him."

"He got our leader killed," Zyra argued. "He owes us a debt."

"Then I'll repay the debt." She reached into her pocket. "I have three coins, and a dagger, and—"

"That's not how this works," Sparrow said apathetically.

Zyra stepped closer to Jemma. "He hurt our guild. Now he needs to help our guild."

"Or die," Sparrow chimed in.

"He's your friend!" Jemma yelled at Sparrow.

"I don't have friends."

Jemma shook her head. "No. Don't hurt him. Whatever help you need to repay the debt, I'll do it. I'll do whatever you want as long as you leave him alone."

Zyra looked up in thought, still keeping her grip on Jemma's arm. Jemma winced as fingernails dug into her skin. She impatiently awaited her judgement, desperately hoping that it wouldn't result in the death of her friend, but to her surprise, Sparrow spoke before Zyra.

"Send her on Kinsley's quest," Sparrow said.

Zyra chuckled. "That's letting them off easy. You're getting soft," Zyra said, which earned her a harsh glare from Sparrow, "but it's not a bad idea."

"What is Kinsley's quest?" Jemma asked.

"It's an opportunity for you to keep Callum alive," Sparrow told her.

"I'll have the details of the quest for you tomorrow," Zyra said. "Complete the task, and Callum's debt will be repaid."

Jemma sat in the corner of the guild floor—her new home for the night—and eavesdropped on the conversations. With Ash gone, they had to find a new guild leader, which no one could agree upon. After much debate and compromise, they elected Zyra temporarily until they could decide on a more permanent solution. Slowly, people trickled out of the building. Sparrow put out the lamps and left without a word. Jemma was left alone in the dark, hugging her knees, tears streaming down her face. She hoped Callum's hiding spot was good enough to keep him safe.

Jemma jumped at the sound of footsteps in the dark. "Who's there?" she asked.

"It's me." She felt a piece of fabric hit her in the face. "Do you want a blanket?" Scraps asked.

"Sure." She gently accepted the gift from him. "Thank you."

"Goodnight," Scraps said as his footsteps shied away.

Derek

It was too early in the morning to be awake.

The sun was still below the horizon; the sky was lit with only a few stray rays, yet Torin had insisted that they needed to go hunting. Derek knew it wasn't necessary—they still had plenty of venison remaining from yesterday's hunt—but he followed Torin out into the woods nonetheless. Waking up earlier than the sun was less painful than arguing with his older brother. They perched in one of their typical chosen spots, waiting for an unlucky woodland animal to wander by.

Torin took a deep breath. "Do you ever think about... um..."

"I thought hunting was supposed to be a silent activity." Derek repeated back the principle that Torin had drilled into him.

"Right." Torin became quiet.

"Do I ever think about what?" Derek asked.

Torin chuckled. "Do you ever think about how no girl would ever date you?"

"No, but I often think about how they'd never date you," Derek shot back.

Torin didn't laugh or argue or punch. He sat still in silence again.

"That wasn't what you were originally going to say, though," Derek pointed out.

Torin shook his head.

Derek elbowed his brother. "Come on. Tell me."

Torin elbowed him back harder.

Derek rolled his eyes and returned to silence, watching the wind attack the leaves, watching the clouds wander across the sky.

Hunting was boring.

He looked over at his brother. Torin, who typically found a strange peace in waiting to kill an animal, now looked anxious.

"Out with it. Now," Derek insisted.

"You don't get to make demands of me," Torin argued.

"I'll fight you for it. If I win, you talk. If you win, I..." He had to think of a suitable trade. "I'll give you twenty gold coins."

"Where are you going to get that? You don't even have a job."

Twenty gold coins was the typical prize for *losing* a fight. "I have my secrets."

"Are you a thief?"

"No, Torin. You have such little faith in me."

Torin tossed his bow aside, took off his quiver, and stood up. He balled his hands into fists. "Fine. Let's go."

With a grin, Derek punched his brother in the face. He immediately regretted it—not the fight, but how hard he punched. He didn't mind hurting Torin, but he didn't want to reveal his secret. He had grown a lot stronger in the past year of ring fights, while Torin didn't fight anyone but his own younger siblings. It could be an easy win, if Derek tried, but he didn't. He let Torin get a few punches in here and there, intentionally failing to block, and pretended to falter or stumble a few times. In the end, still, he won. He didn't want his brother to know his strength, but he did want to know what his brother was thinking about.

Derek pinned Torin face down in the dirt. "Alright, I win. Give up already." After a bit of useless struggling, Torin tapped out, and Derek let him up. "Now tell me what you're thinking about."

Torin wiped the dirt off his face. "The spring festival is next week."

Now they both sat in silence, neither wanting to speak their thoughts.

"Tara was supposed to be watching them," Torin finally said.

"She was thirteen," Derek said.

"And they were eleven and nine," Torin shot back. "They couldn't protect themselves. Tara let them die."

"Tara was *thirteen*," Derek re-emphasized, "and while Mom and Dad were grieving, who was placed in charge of the other five kids? Tara was. She was a child tasked with looking after five children, and then Mom and Dad added a sixth. I stepped up to help her. You disappeared."

Torin laughed. "That's what you think happened?"

"That's exactly what happened."

Torin grabbed his bow and his quiver. "I didn't know you could be so clueless," Torin said as he wandered further into the woods. "Go help Tara take the kids to school," he shouted over his shoulder. "I can handle this on my own."

Elijah

Elijah lifted the sword, running his fingers over the simple design engraved in the hilt. It felt lighter than he remembered—he had been much younger and smaller the last time he had held it—yet it was heavier than he expected. It was, after all, a weapon—one that relied on momentum to be effective—so the logic of its weight could be easily explained, yet the emotions weighed more than the sword itself. It felt fragile, as if damaging the weapon would somehow tarnish his dad's memory. It felt burdensome, as if it came with expectations, as if the sword itself would be angry at the failures of its wielder. Above it all, it felt compelling. Eli swiped at the air with the sword, spinning as he took a few steps forward, attacking nonexistent enemies. He remembered his father's stories. Whether reality or legend, they were inspiring; they told of friendship and adventure, of justice and leadership, and of finding the last glimpse of hope in the midst of defeat. Eli swung the sword again, piercing invisible creatures, slicing imaginary monsters. He paused with the sword over his shoulder and set it down with a sigh. This was stupid. He looked like Tobias on the playground with a stick.

He returned to reality and headed out of his house. It was time to pick his son up from school.

Jareth

"Jareth, where is your father? It's getting late." Jareth's mom looked out the window, watching, waiting, staring into the sunset.

"He won't be home for a few days," Jareth said. He was desperately counting down those days.

"A few more days? Why does it take so long?"

"He's on a boat, Mom."

His mom turned to look at him. "A boat? Why would he be on a boat?"

Jareth sighed. He couldn't stand to watch her like this. She needed a cure, and she needed it soon. He grabbed his spell book off the shelf and tossed his backpack over his shoulder. "Mom, I need to go meet up with a friend. Will you stay here?"

"Where else would I go?"

Jareth gave his mom a quick hug on his way out the door. "I love you, Mom. I'll be back soon."

The walk to Reece's tavern felt longer than ever. Jareth dragged his feet along the dirt road, past familiar locals and a few lost tourists. He heard the tavern long before he saw it; the live music blared across the entire shoreline.

Jareth pushed through the crowd to reach the bar where Reece was drying glasses and keeping an eye on the customers. He chuckled as Jareth approached. "You ditched me yesterday. What sort of trouble did you get yourself into?"

Jareth stared back with tired eyes.

"You're not the type to get yourself into trouble. That's normally Jemma and Callum, but... I haven't seen them in a while."

"They went to Illia. I figured you knew."

Reece froze. "You're kidding."

Jareth shrugged. "That's what they told me."

Reece shook his head. "Let's hope they make it back alive." He tossed the towel over his shoulder and set the glass in his hand on the shelf with the others. He pointed to Jareth's spell book. "What are you trying to learn now?"

"We need to skip to healing spells."

Reece chuckled. "You don't just skip to healing spells."

"We need to." Jareth flipped through the pages of the book to reach the last chapter. "I've looked at the healing spells before, but they've never made any sense. I—"

"Healing spells are a myth, Jareth."

"What do you mean?" Jareth asked in confusion. He looked down at the spells that clearly existed.

"They're impossible to master. They're the last chapter in that book for a reason. Besides, they're not that useful when medicine exists."

"Medicine can't fix this," Jareth said. "I need magic."

"Sit down," Reece instructed. He handed Jareth a drink.

Jareth took a sip and almost choked. "That wasn't water this time."

"You sound like you need something stronger than water." Reece grabbed a stool and sat across from Jareth, propping his elbows on the bar. "Why do you need healing spells? Is it Abigail?"

"No, it's..." He paused, lost in his own thoughts. Why hadn't he thought of curing Abigail with magic? He had been too selfish, too worried about his mother, to even think about the dying child. "Can we use magic to cure Abigail?"

Reece shook his head. "I've already tried. Whatever is wrong with her, it's bad. I don't think she'll make it to Caridelle."

"Did you tell that to Clarissa?"

"No. That girl has been through enough." Reece sighed. "Who are you trying to heal?"

"My mom. She's starting to lose her memory. She still remembers me, but sometimes she thinks I'm in school, and she forgets where my dad is, and—"

"There's not a spell to fix that, Jareth."

"There must be," Jareth insisted.

"There's not," Reece said. "Healing spells—which, as I said, are impossible to master anyways—are for curing stab wounds and reattaching limbs. They can't stop the effects of old age. That's just part of life."

Jareth stared at the book. What had been the point of learning magic if it couldn't accomplish his singular goal? He had only started studying magic in the first place to help his mom, and yet, he had failed. The best thing he could do now was return home and make sure she hadn't wandered into trouble.

He closed the book and slid it towards Reece. "Here. You can have it. I don't need it anymore."

Reece slid it back. "Keep it. Magic can't solve all your problems, but it's far from useless. You never know when you'll need it."

Jareth took the book. "I should go home."

"Come back tomorrow. I want to work on some attack spells," Reece said.

"We'll see," Jareth responded as he stepped out of the tavern and into the cold dark night.

Jemma

It was her second night on the road, and Jemma still couldn't figure out how to set up a tent.

Tents were Callum's job. He was the calm and casual one. She was the sneaky and deceptive thief. Unless she could steal a person who knew how to set up a tent, her talents were being severely underutilized.

Eventually, just like the night before, she gave up. She tossed the tent to the side and slept in the grass.

A cold sprinkle of rain woke her in the middle of the night. She pulled the tent canvas over herself and went back to sleep, hoping it wouldn't suffocate her in her slumber.

Illia was still close, only a two-day walk away. She could always return; it was a tempting offer, but for Callum, she'd find a way to travel to the moon and back.

Zyra had insisted she needed a team, yet refused to lend her any guild personnel. Considering that Zyra had also banned her from finding help in Illia, Mistcoast was Jemma's best bet for recruiting people.

Zyra, out of spite, had enjoyed making Jemma's quest more difficult.

As the sun rose, the rain finally gave Jemma a break. Her long day of walking gave her plenty of time to think. Illia wasn't too far behind her. She could still give up, return to Zyra and Sparrow, and become a member of the thieves' guild, living relatively comfortably and never setting foot in Mistcoast again—all at the expense of Callum's life. Despite the appealing option, her feet continued away from Illia. She had never worried about anyone but herself, much less gone through this much trouble to rescue them from their own mistakes. Why was Callum any different?

Best friend. The words echoed in her mind. Callum had called her his *best friend.* Technically, Storm had called Sky that, and it was all part of their spy mission. Still, when Callum had said it, it didn't feel like a lie.

Jemma had never really considered anyone a friend. She didn't know what friendship was supposed to look like. But if it meant doing something reckless to rescue someone from their own mistakes, maybe she was doing this friendship thing right.

Clarissa

Time passed slowly yet way too fast. Clarissa only had a week left with the kids. She cherished every moment despite the pain and chaos, yet the seconds slipped away like grains of sand falling through her fingers. There was nothing she could do to make the week last longer.

She sat on the floor surrounded by kids, helping them with their homework. It was difficult to jump between teaching complex math and basic shapes and colors, but with Eloise's help, she managed. She'd had a lot of practice in the past few months.

"Clarissa, I figured it out! The answer is four!" Tristan shouted proudly.

Clarissa walked over and looked at the problem. 100 divided by 25 was indeed 4. "Good job, Tristan."

"Clarissa, what is this word?" Owen asked, holding up his book.

"That says 'water'. That's not even hard," Charlette said.

"Charlette, be nice," Eloise said. "He's only seven."

"And I'm only eight!"

"Reading is hard," Owen complained, slamming his book down on the table.

"You can do hard things," Clarissa told him, repeating one of her mom's favorite phrases. She sat at the table beside him and opened up his book. "What's this word?" She helped him sound out the words and put together the phrases. She was going to miss these moments.

She still hadn't found a home for Owen, Melody, and Lucas, but she had found homes for the others. It felt wrong picking which kids went with which families. She didn't feel like she should be deciding their futures, yet someone had to make the decision, and she did the best she could.

"Clarissa?" Eloise asked as she finished reading the book with Owen.

"Do you need help with your homework too?" Clarissa teased.

Eloise shook her head. "It's our last week before graduation. They don't really make us do any homework."

"Lucky you."

Eloise clasped her hands behind her back. "They had a career fair at school today," she said, a hint of hesitation in her voice that caught Clarissa off guard.

"How did that go?" Clarissa asked.

Eloise smiled. "I have an interview tomorrow."

"That's great!" Clarissa shouted with excitement. "Are you excited? Are you nervous?"

Eloise's eyes dropped to the ground. "I feel bad that I won't be able to help you with the kids tomorrow after school, but—"

"Eloise." Clarissa stood up and placed her hands on Eloise's shoulders, refusing to speak until Eloise made eye contact. "It's not your responsibility to take care of these kids. It never was. You helped out of the kindness of your heart, and I appreciate that, but don't put the weight of that on your shoulders, okay?"

Clarissa nodded, and Eloise nodded in return.

"Have fun at your interview. You're one of the smartest people I know. They'd be lucky to hire you."

Eloise nodded. "I will." She hugged Clarissa tight. "Clarissa?"

"Yes, Eloise?"

"It was never your responsibility either."

Derek

"Trevor, wake up."

"Five more minutes, Derek," Trevor begged as he pulled his blanket over his head.

"Nope." Derek stole the blanket and walked out of the room, ignoring the protests from his little brother. He entered the living room, where Tara stood waiting with Nora and Tegan.

"Is he coming?" Tara asked.

"He'll be ready in a minute," Derek said, tossing the blanket onto the couch.

Torin stepped through the front door holding a bow. "Derek, hurry up." He glanced around the living room at the scattered toys and blankets and dishes before making eye contact with Tara. "Clean this up."

Tara scoffed. "I'm taking the kids to school," she said.

"Then do it while they're at school," Torin said, already turning to walk out the door.

"I have other responsibilities, unlike you," Tara argued.

"Not this again," Torin muttered.

"Tegan's not old enough to go to school, but you probably don't pay enough attention to even know that. And Mom's busy today, so I have to watch Tegan and Alec while you go wander around the woods—"

Her angry rant was interrupted by the loud slam of the door.

Tegan tugged on Tara's hand. "What's wrong?"

Tara sighed and shook her head. "Nothing, Tegan."

Derek glared at the closed door where his brother had just stood.

"It's fine," Tara told him.

He shook his head. "It's not."

A minute later, Trevor entered the room, his eyes half closed, dragging his school backpack behind him. As Tara escorted the young kids outside, Derek headed to find his brother.

Torin shot an arrow at a target, hitting the bullseye on his first try. "Are you here for archery practice, or are you here to complain like Tara?" he said. Apparently, he didn't need to turn around to know his brother was approaching from behind him.

"Tara's right, you know?"

"Seriously?" Torin tossed aside the bow and turned to face his brother. "Are we really going to hash this out again? When will you let this go?"

Derek's eyes narrowed. "When you learn to respect my little sister."

"She's my little sister, too."

"Then treat her like it," Derek demanded. "I know she was supposed to be watching Thomas and Devin the day of the festival. I know she ditched us for a year. She's not perfect, but she and I work our butts off every day in that house while you're running off to who-knows-where."

Torin chuckled. "You're so lucky to live your life in ignorance."

"You keep saying that!" Derek shouted. "Are you ever going to actually tell me what that means?"

"You really want to know?" Torin asked, taking a step towards Derek. "It means that while you've been busy playing hopscotch, I've been busy putting food on the table. While you've been cleaning the house, I've been making sure we don't lose the house. Who do you think pays the mortgage, Derek?" Torin paused, waiting for an answer.

Derek froze. "Dad—"

"Dad hasn't held a stable job since Thomas and Devin died. I've been the one working nights to pay for the mortgage. Stop complaining that I'm not there to tuck the kids into bed!" Torin drew nearer to Derek as he spoke, squeezing his hands into tight fists. "I'm the one who dragged Dad out of bed in the deepest points of his depression. I'm the one Mom came crying to in her grief. While you've been busy taking care of the kids, I've been busy taking care of our parents, and the house, and the food, and..." His voice trailed off with sorrow, but his fists and his jaw were clenched with rage.

For once, Derek couldn't find a quippy remark. He watched his brother with sadness, confusion, and the tiniest bit of pity.

"Don't give me that look," Torin said, turning away.

A moment of silence passed before Derek spoke. "Why did you never tell me any of this?"

Torin sighed. "You and Tara can sit and talk about your feelings all day, but I think it's worthless. I'd rather go do something," Torin said as he picked up his bow.

"Like target practice?" Derek asked as he picked up his own weapon. His mind raced with questions, but he'd be pushing his luck with Torin if he asked any.

"Like target practice," Torin said as he drew his bow.

Elijah

The waves were calm, and the skies were clear. Elijah sat in his small boat, floating on the gentle waves. The conditions should have been relaxing, yet Elijah's mind flooded with anxiety. The still water let the stupid fish see his every move and avoid getting caught.

He couldn't sell fish if he couldn't catch any.

He couldn't make money to provide for his son if he had nothing to sell.

His son, luckily, never asked for much more than hugs and attention. He never complained when they ran low on food or when he couldn't have the toys his friends at school had. Yet somehow, Tobias's contentment only made Elijah feel worse. His son deserved the world, and he could give him nothing more than a small sliver of Mistcoast.

Anna could have given him so much more. She was witty and smart, with a great sense of humor. She would have taught Tobias so much more than Elijah ever could. She was strong-willed and passionate with every opinion she had, whether it was her deeply held beliefs about humanity or her preference for red clothing over any other color. She loved in a way that was intentional and personal; she kept a small group of close friends instead of a larger group of acquaintances. Still, she'd gladly ditch them any day to spend time with her husband, her best friend. Their relationship was great until it wasn't. As Eli's thoughts wandered to memories of his wife, he caught himself subconsciously humming her lullaby. He stopped himself as soon as he noticed. It brought too many memories and too much pain.

He shielded his eyes with his hand and looked towards the sun. School would be over soon.

With his bucket devoid of fish, he rowed back towards the shore. He didn't have dinner for the kid, but he could send Tobias to Sophia's home for the evening. His sister would succeed where he had failed.

Jareth

Mr. Campbell was going to kill him.

For the first time, Jareth had missed work. He had tried to leave the house, but his mom insisted on walking him to school, and when he tried to explain reality, she only became more confused. He was too scared to leave her alone. Instead, he told her it was a weekend—a lie she believed despite her denial of every truth—and they stayed home all day playing card games. She was excited to spend time with her son, and Jareth was grateful for an excuse to keep an eye on her.

His mom laid down four aces. "I win!" she announced with excitement. Jareth gave her a smile, clearly fake, but she was as gullible as little Abigail.

"I'm tired, Jareth. I'm going to go to sleep. Stay up as long as you want, but make sure you do your homework." She kissed him on the forehead and limped towards her room.

Jareth grabbed his spell book and flipped through the back pages. Despite the magic outlined inside, the book itself was simply ink and paper. The spells in the back hadn't miraculously changed; there were still no answers about how to heal his mom.

He couldn't heal her, but he could take care of her to the best of his ability. He might get fired, but at least his mom would be happy and healthy. He glanced at the calendar on the wall. In four days, his father would return to help. Hopefully, he still had his job by then.

As the sun set, he didn't bother to light a lantern. He sat on the couch in dark silence. Crickets chirped at him through the thin walls, and starlight peeked through the windows. He ran his fingers across the distressed leather cover of his book, feeling every bend and scratch from its travels. He wondered how many others had held this old book and wished the world were different than it was. This book was full of answers to plenty of problems, but not his. Maybe, despite what school had led him to believe, there wasn't an answer to every question.

A knock at the door broke through the silence. He answered it to see Reece.

"Shouldn't you be working?" Jareth asked.

Reece shook his head. "The bar is closed already."

"The sun has barely set."

Reece stared at the stars above him. "Looks like the sun disappeared hours ago," Reece noted before returning his attention to Jareth. "Why'd you miss work today?"

"How'd you know?"

Reece shrugged. "I know everything."

"Who told you?"

"Mr. Ellis. He tried to come by your store today, and it was closed."

Jareth sighed. "Well, my mom—"

"You don't have to make excuses, Jareth," Reece interrupted. "I just came to make sure you're alive and maybe teach you some magic."

"Are you really going to throw Knife spells at me right now?"

Reece shook his head. "You need a distraction, but that's too harsh."

Jareth pushed the door open. "Fine. Come inside, but you have to be quiet. My mom's asleep."

Reece grinned. "Perfect. We can work on telepathic messaging."

Clarissa

Clarissa sorted through the kids' art projects. Tiny handprints filled tiny pages, becoming turkeys or flowers or trees or spiders. It was amazing how many shapes teachers could turn a handprint into. She sorted their drawings into piles, from Abigail's little scribbles to Lucas's beautiful landscapes. One picture of a sailboat on the ocean caught her eye. She remembered those days, when twelve-year-old Lucas used to sit by the shore and draw. Now, someone had convinced fourteen-year-old Lucas that art wasn't "cool". She hoped his new family could convince him otherwise.

She finished with art and moved on to clothes. They'd been passing down clothes from kid to kid for so long that it was hard to identify what belonged to whom. Owen's clothes had been passed down from Tristan, and Melody's clothes had once been worn by Jemma and Eloise. She sorted them the best she could and packed them into any bag she found lying around.

Her peaceful afternoon of organization was interrupted by children pouring through the front door. "Look what I made today!" Owen said. He held up a painting of red thumbprints with green lines below.

"Wow! That's beautiful, Owen!" She squatted to his level and looked at the painting. She tried her best to comprehend the mess of red and green but failed to decipher the image.

"Flowers," Eloise said quietly.

"I love the flowers, Owen," Clarissa said.

"Our teacher told us to draw flowers for the festival!"

"Shut up, Owen," Lucas said.

"Hey, leave him alone!" Melody argued.

"He's the one who brought up the festival! Why would he even bring that up?"

"He's seven!"

"He's old enough to know better!"

"He's too young to remember," Cosette whispered.

"You're too young to remember too," Lucas said. "You're lucky."

"We're old enough to remember that you become a jerk every year during it," Charlette said.

"Enough," Clarissa demanded. "That's enough. We're done talking about the festival."

"I don't even want to go to that stupid thing," Lucas said.

"Then don't," Clarissa told him. "You're 14. Stay home if you want, but don't ruin Owen's fun."

As the arguments settled down and the kids dragged out their toys, Eloise approached Clarissa. "Do you remember that interview I mentioned?"

Clarissa nodded. "Of course! How'd it go?"

"I got the job," Eloise said with a hesitant smile.

"Of course you did!" Clarissa hugged her excitedly. "What's the job? When do you start?"

"Right after the festival ends."

"That's quick," Clarissa responded. The graduation ceremony lined up with the yearly spring festival; she was surprised they were putting her to work only a day after her graduation.

"I'll need to pack up my stuff before then," Eloise informed her. "I should probably go ahead and start."

"You know, I didn't touch your stuff when I started packing. You're basically an adult now. You can go wherever you want, but you're welcome to stay here at the orphanage while you start your job."

"Well, that's the thing..." Eloise wrung her hands.

"Where's the job taking you?" Clarissa asked as she pieced the situation together.

Eloise's grin widened. "Everywhere. I get to work on a boat. Our first trip is to Laresse, and after that, we'll go wherever the contracts take us. They said they'll teach me everything I need to know."

"That's amazing." Clarissa hugged Eloise tight, her best friend, the closest thing she had to a sister. Tears welled up in her eyes.

Eloise laughed. "Please don't cry," she pleaded as she held back her own tears.

"Your mom would be so proud," Clarissa told her. "My mom would be proud too."

"I'll come visit every time I'm in Mistcoast. I can bring back presents for you and Abigail."

Clarissa glanced back at the closed door to the room where Abigail still lay sleeping. "She'll love that."

Jemma

Jemma ran as fast as her legs would allow for hours on end until her knees gave way. She abandoned her puzzling tent and slept in the trees instead. Any tree could be her treehouse if it was big enough to hold her. Her feet pounded the dirt road. She didn't need to run—Zyra had given her plenty of time to complete the quest—but there was nothing else to do. Ruminating on her circumstance accomplished nothing, but running brought her to her destination faster. She poured every ounce of energy into her steps.

Callum would be okay. She had decided it was true. She would complete the quest—simply steal a box of scrolls from the Red Coin and deliver them to Kinsley in Caridelle—and her best friend would be saved. It was the only option. She couldn't imagine losing him, and she'd had lots of days traveling to imagine it. She couldn't envision her life alone, without Callum or Sparrow or Ash or even Zyra to keep her company. Where would she even settle without friends to guide her movements? Would she become a nomad, wandering from place to place in search of something unknown?

She scolded herself for considering the possibility. There was no time and energy for thinking. All she could do was sprint. She ran towards the place she hated for the person she loved.

DEREK

Derek waited impatiently outside of his house. He was going to be late for his fight if his little sister didn't hurry up. She had walked out of the house with him only seconds ago, but ran suddenly back inside, insisting she had forgotten something.

Tara returned with a small box. "I'm ready now!"

"What's that?"

"Cookies."

"Why? So you have a snack while you watch me fight?"

"No, so that Kane has a snack while we watch you fight."

"You baked cookies for Kane," Derek said in disbelief.

"Yes." She tilted her head in confusion. "Why? Do you think Kane doesn't like cookies?"

"I'm sure he likes cookies, but—"

"Good. I can't date a guy who doesn't like cookies. Come on." She hurried through the trees, tugging on Derek's arm behind her.

Derek let her drag him along, trying to strategize what to do about Kane. He didn't mind his sister going on dates, but he wished she had picked someone easier to beat up.

The arena was already packed by the time they arrived. Kane found them immediately. "Hey, Derek," Kane said. He smiled. "Hey, Tara."

"Do you like cookies?" Tara asked.

"Sure. Why?"

She held out the box proudly. "I brought you cookies."

He chuckled and tousled her hair. "You're cute."

"Alright, I have to go punch someone," Derek said before walking off. Part of him wanted to supervise his sister's little date, and another part of him wanted to gag every time they spoke.

He stood in the back corner and wrapped bandages around his hands, sizing up his opponent across the room. The guy smirked with fake confidence as his friends hyped him up. He looked like a traveler—not a local. This would be an easy win.

Derek entered the fighting ring, glancing over at his sister. Her eyes met his, and a smile crossed her face. He read her expression easily. She was expecting him to win. She sat at a table alone, the chair across empty. Derek's eyes scanned the room until he found Kane talking to a couple of his friends whom he employed to help organize the fights. To Derek's own surprise, he wished Kane were distracting his sister at the moment. He'd never get used to his sister watching him get beat up.

The first punch came before he even noticed his opponent had entered the ring. The referee hadn't started the fight yet, but this guy either didn't know the rules or didn't care. Derek punched back, restraining his full force. He could beat this guy quickly, but he prolonged the fight to give the crowd a good show.

He punched once, twice, a third time. His opponent punched him back in the nose. He wiped the blood from his face, smearing the white bandages on his fists with red. The crowd cheered him on, but his sister's voice broke through the noise. "Come on, Derek! You've got this!"

He tried to knock the guy off balance but failed. He'd have to try a little harder. He threw more punches as distractions before he tried to knock down his opponent again. His sister's voice broke through the crowd again, but this time, instead of cheering, he heard irritated shouting. Something was wrong.

As he turned to look at his sister, his opponent took the opportunity to tackle him, slamming his head into the ground. He winced in pain and squeezed his eyes shut. That was going to leave a bruise. As he shoved away his opponent, he finally got a look at Tara. She had stood up from the table and was arguing with someone. It took Derek a moment to make out the figure in the chaos, but he eventually deciphered who it was: Torin.

He stepped out of the ring and tried to make his way through the crowd. His opponent didn't seem to get the memo, following him out of the ring and still trying to fight. "Dude, stop it." Derek turned around, blocked a punch, and shoved the guy to the ground. He landed on the wood floor and looked at Derek in confusion. Derek glared back. "Fight's over. Leave me alone."

Kane reached Tara faster than Derek could, drawing plenty of attention as the head of the fighting ring. Everyone now turned to face the argument between Kane and Tara and Torin, huddling closer to get a view of the drama, making it increasingly difficult for Derek to reach his sister.

"Let me through!" Derek insisted, pushing his way through the crowd. He could finally hear their discussion as he neared his siblings.

"—can't just leave the house like that!" Torin shouted. "You're too irresponsible to even—"

"I can leave whenever I want," Tara said as Kane placed a gentle hand on her back. "I'm an adult."

"Who's this guy?" Torin looked at Kane. "Just another stranger to have a baby with?"

"Torin, stop!" Derek shouted as he tried to push through the crowd.

"You're embarrassing me! Just leave!" Tara shoved Torin back towards the door, and Derek winced. He knew Torin well enough to know what would come next—his sister's scream as Torin's fist hit her—but that scream never came.

Kane caught Torin's fist and glared at him. The crowd immediately hushed. "I'm the one who organizes fights around here. You don't get to just walk into this place and start punching."

Derek finally managed to break through the crowd, placing himself between his little sister and older brother. "Get out of here, Torin."

Torin redirected his aggression from Tara to Derek. "Seriously? You're out here getting beat up for money, Tara's out here dating guys twice her age—"

"He's twenty-five!" Tara argued, but Torin didn't stop.

"—and you expect me to just sit back and watch it happen?"

"I expect you to not punch your little sister in the face," Derek said.

"And I expected you to protect her. Instead, you let her make all the stupid decisions she wants."

"I am protecting her," Derek argued, "from you."

"Leave." Kane glared at Torin. "This is your last warning."

Torin hesitated, as if he truly had a choice, but ultimately turned and left. "We'll talk about this when you two get home," he said before slamming the door on his way out.

"Are you okay?" Kane asked Tara.

She shrugged. "I'm fine. I'm pretty used to it."

Kane shook his head. "There's something wrong with your family."

Tara laughed. "I know."

Mumbles spread through the crowd. People weren't sure whether the fighting was over, but Kane's voice broke the awkward silence. "Move on to the next fight. Derek's not fighting anyone else tonight."

As the next fight began and the commotion resumed, Kane subtly pulled Derek aside, but Tara followed. "Where are we going?" she asked.

"I need to talk with your brother," Kane told her.

Tara crossed her arms. "Anything you say to him you can say to me."

Derek sighed. "Tara, seriously, can you give us a minute?"

Tara rolled her eyes. "You're acting like Torin now."

Derek's eyebrows raised.

"Okay, that was too far," she admitted. She tossed her hands up in surrender. "I'll leave you two alone."

Derek kept an eye on his sister as she walked away. He'd trust her with his life, but he didn't for a second trust her not to eavesdrop. Once she was seated at a table on the other side of the room, Derek turned his attention to Kane. "What?"

Kane talked to Derek without taking his eyes off Tara. "She can't go home. Torin will kill her. I'm telling you, not her, so you don't think I'm trying to coerce her into going somewhere else, but—"

"You're right," Derek said. "I mean, Torin won't kill her, but she won't leave unscathed. I can go get a bag of her stuff."

"You won't leave unscathed either," Kane said.

Derek shrugged. "I can take it."

"This isn't a joke, Derek." Kane finally took his eyes off Tara and looked at Derek. "She can't go back there. Torin hasn't fully snapped yet. One of these days, he's going to cause wounds that won't heal."

"Thanks for pointing out the obvious, Kane, but do you have a solution? There's nowhere else for her to go."

"She can always stay here," Kane offered.

"You want her to sleep on the wooden floor of a fighting ring all night? That won't go over well, especially with Alec."

"Who's Alec?"

"The baby?" Derek laughed at the look on Kane's face. "She conveniently left that part out, didn't she?"

"I don't care," Kane said. "She can bring the kid with her."

"Torin will find her here eventually."

"That's why we get her on a boat to Laresse."

"Do you have the money for that?"

"I was hoping you did."

Derek shook his head. "She won't leave you behind. She gets too easily attached."

"Then I'll go."

Derek chuckled. "You'd leave Mistcoast behind for her?"

"I'd burn down Mistcoast for her." Kane glanced over at Tara again, then turned back to see Derek's concerned face. "Now that was a joke. Calm down."

"I'll get the money," Derek promised. "I'll get enough to send her and Alec and you, if she wants you to come."

"What about yourself?" Kane asked.

"I'll figure it out. Maybe I'll come, but if not, I need you to convince her to leave me behind."

"That's a difficult task, Derek."

Derek shrugged. "As is getting the coin to send three people across the ocean," he said over his shoulder as he walked away. He weaved back through the crowd to sit beside his sister.

She grinned at him. "Thanks for not beating up my boyfriend."

"I'm saving that fight for later," Derek teased.

She leaned her head on his shoulder. "Why is family such a mess?"

Derek shrugged. "That's just how it is," he said, yet he refused to accept that. He wouldn't let Tara live in this mess any longer. All he had to do was earn enough money to ship her across the ocean—and convince her to get on the boat.

Elijah

“Can I come fishing with you today?” Tobias begged.

“You have school.”

“But fishing!”

“Later,” Elijah insisted.

“Tomorrow?”

“You have school tomorrow too.”

“We get out early,” Tobias reminded him.

Elijah sighed. The kid was right, and Eli had completely forgotten. Tomorrow was the graduation ceremony and the start of the spring festival. “Maybe we can go fishing on Saturday.” He’d need something to distract him from the upcoming anniversary. “Today you have to go to school though.”

“I don’t want to.”

“Tobias. You have to go to school.”

“Please?”

“Is this about the festival again?”

Tobias nodded. “My teachers won’t stop talking about it, and Cosette is always crying about it.”

“Who is Cosette?”

“The cute girl, Dad! I told you this already.”

“Right, the cute girl.” He had been hoping Tobias would forget about that. “Well, maybe you need to be at school today to give her a hug when she’s crying.” Eli cringed internally at his own words. He couldn’t believe he was encouraging an eight-year-old’s primary school crush.

"Fine, I'll go to school." Tobias hugged his dad before running off towards the playground.

Eli headed quickly towards the docks. Normally, on a nice day like this, he would have considered taking Tobias with him, but today, he couldn't afford to risk his productivity. They were running low on food, and Eli was tired of borrowing money from his sister. He needed to catch double the fish: some to eat, and some to sell. Clarissa would probably gladly overpay again for anything he caught, although that income source was about to end as soon as she dismantled the orphanage.

He hopped into his boat and began rowing out to sea. The sunlight reflected beautifully off the waves, and a few large boats floated in the distance. Once he was far enough away from the shore, Elijah cast a line and rested in his boat, watching the landscape. He had always felt like he belonged in the village of Mistcoast, but it was here on the waves that he felt most at home. Throughout the day, however, this feeling of home faded as his frustration grew. The fish seemed to read his every move and knew to avoid him no matter which bait he used and no matter which spot he picked. Over the course of hours, he tried every technique he knew, but nothing seemed to work.

He rowed back to shore at the end of the school day with only a couple miniscule fish to cook for dinner. Cohen was waiting for him on the dock. Eli tossed him a rope to help moor the boat.

"You're still late on your payment, and you're about to owe a second one," Cohen reprimanded as he tied a knot in the rope.

Eli sighed. "I'm well aware. I'm doing everything I can. I'll have both payments to you soon. I just need you to wait a little longer."

"My boss is tired of waiting."

"Can't you convince him to cut me some slack?"

"I already did," Cohen sighed. "He's given you some grace multiple times in the past year, and he's refusing to do it again. He's taking the boat back."

Elijah froze. Cohen couldn't be serious.

"I'm sorry, Eli. It's not my choice."

"I need the boat to make money, and I need money to pay for the boat," Eli explained as he stepped onto the dock. "What am I supposed to do?"

"Find another way to make money," Cohen said. "I have a ship repair job for you tonight."

"That's not enough to catch up on payments."

"I know, but it's something. Do you want it or not?" He held out a paper with the repair details written on it, and Elijah took it from him. "I can't do anything about it, Eli. Trust me; I tried everything I could," Cohen said. He stood still, watching, as Eli continued his normal end-of-day routine with the boat. "Eli?" he finally spoke again. He waited until Eli met his eyes to say the last sentence before leaving. "I'm sorry."

Eli glanced back at the boat. It was tempting to steal it, but what good would that do? The little rowboat wouldn't last a night in the waves of the deep ocean. It wasn't made to travel the world; it was made to float along the shoreline of Mistcoast, never to leave far from its home. It wasn't much different from Anna's boat, which disappeared the same day she did.

Without realizing it again, he started humming her lullaby, the one Tobias had been begging him to sing for weeks. A stanza in, he stopped humming. It never sounded right in his own voice. Instead, he imagined the song in his head in Anna's voice. It had always sounded better when his wife sang it; Tobias had refused to sleep when Elijah sang the lullaby. Anna's voice sounded like the sunrise, and Elijah's sounded like the rippled and muddied reflection of the sun on the ocean's surface. It was nothing but a cheap imitation of the real song.

Elijah glanced back at the boat as he walked away, saying goodbye to the only place he truly felt at peace.

Jareth

"Why aren't you in school, Jareth?" his mom asked again. "Shouldn't you be going to school? I don't want you to be late."

"I won't be late," Jareth said as he stared at the calendar. It wouldn't be long until his father returned home. As of tomorrow, he would have some help caring for his mom. Still, that wouldn't solve all the issues. His dad's return wouldn't suddenly heal his mom, and inevitably, his dad would have to depart on another work trip after a couple of weeks home, leaving Jareth to again try to juggle caring for his mom with a full-time job.

He grabbed his backpack. "I'll see you after school," he said as he left for work. Lying felt horrible, but arguing with his confused mother felt even worse.

As he entered the store, he saw his boss, Mr. Campbell, sitting inside already, reading a book. "Good morning," Jareth said hesitantly. The old man looked up from his book with a frown, although Jareth could never tell if the emotion was pointed at him or simply the man's default expression.

"I heard some people came by the store earlier this week and you weren't here."

"I'm sorry, sir. My mom is sick. I stayed home with her."

"You have a job. You need to be here."

Jareth nodded. "It won't happen again," he said, a promise he knew he couldn't keep.

"Good. Clean up this place. It's a mess." Mr. Campbell left without another word.

Jareth looked around the store. Everything was perfectly in its place. The apples could maybe be a little more organized in their pile, but people would just dig through them to find the perfect one anyways. The closest thing to a "mess" was the footprints of dirt that Mr. Campbell tracked in. Jareth swept the floor and unlocked the door for customers. With the spring festival beginning tonight, he expected the store—and the rest of the market—to be bustling. He watched as floral vendors passed by with wheelbarrows full of wildflowers, beautiful colors that would soon decorate the entire village. Customers came flooding in to buy flour and eggs and fruit to bake the traditional pastries. Jareth was excited to get off work and see the town covered in celebratory decorations, yet he planned on keeping the store open longer than usual to make sure every customer had the ingredients they needed.

Around noon, during the peak hours of business, Clarissa joined the crowd inside the store. She waved at Jareth.

"Would you like help gathering everything?" Jareth immediately offered.

"I just need food for me and Abigail for a few days until we run off to Caridelle," Clarissa said, holding up her paper list. "It's a lot shorter of a list than normal."

Jareth watched from his spot behind the counter as Clarissa navigated the store. She was stopped several times by customers who knew her, and she greeted every one with a genuine smile.

'What are you up to?' Reece asked telepathically. Jareth almost jumped out of his seat. Despite practicing the spell a lot recently, Jareth still wasn't used to the sudden voice in his head.

'Working,' Jareth responded in his mind.

'Do you want to learn more magic after work? Would you—'

'Just a minute,' Jareth interrupted Reece's voice in his head as Clarissa approached him with a handful of groceries. She dug in her bag for some coins. "You don't need to pay me," Jareth reminded her.

She sighed. "Are you sure?"

He nodded. "I insist."

She gave him a smile. "Thank you, Jareth," she said before walking out of the store.

'Sorry, I had to talk to Clarissa,' Jareth told Reece.

'Did you tell her how you feel?'

Jareth paused in confusion. 'How do you know about that?'

'It's not hard to figure out,' Reece responded, 'but that's beside the point. Are you free to come to the tavern later?'

Jareth shook his head, then laughed at his own actions when he realized Reece couldn't telepathically see his body language. 'I should probably look after my mom.'

'Understood. If you ever get some free time to practice spells, you know where to find me.'

As Jareth left the store, he had an urge to walk through the center of town, to see all the decorations and explore the festivities as he had in years past. Instead, he walked home. He needed to tell his mom that his day at school had gone well.

Clarissa

Clarissa looked around the orphanage—the place she had called home for the past five years—with a sad smile. Every jacket, every toy, every sentimental treasure had been packed in bags leaned neatly against the wall. For the first time in months, the building was actually clean.

She made their beds for the last time; tomorrow, they'd move to their new homes. The festival would become a time of transition. It was a bit poetic, in a sense, the way the festival had twice moved these kids from one family to the next, yet the first time was caused by tragedy and this time was caused by grace.

Cosette ran through the door excitedly. "School's over! Can I go to the festival?"

"Where are the others?" Clarissa asked.

Cosette's eyes widened. She clasped her hands behind her back and rocked back and forth on her feet. "They already went... I told them to come ask you first, but they didn't listen."

"Stay in the main area of the festival, and try to stick with the older kids. Okay?"

"I will!"

"Then you can go," Clarissa said. Cosette had already disappeared by the time Clarissa had finished her sentence.

Clarissa gently closed the front door that Cosette had left open. When she turned back around, Tristan was now in the room, sitting on the floor against the wall. "I'm not going."

"No one is making you," Clarissa reminded him. "Do you want to talk about—"

"No."

Clarissa nodded. "Okay. I'm going to go check on Abigail."

Abigail smiled at Clarissa as she walked in. Clarissa smiled back. "You're awake."

"I'm awake and I'm bored, Miss Clarissa. I've been bored for days!"

"Well, what do you want to do?"

"Go to the festival," Abigail said. She held up her plush rabbit. "He wants to go to the festival too."

Clarissa shook her head. "You can barely get out of bed, Abigail. You can't go to the festival."

"Can you at least bring me back some flowers?"

"Well, I'm going to stay here tonight with you, but I'll make sure you get flowers before the festival is over."

"Thanks." Abigail weakly hugged Clarissa before lying back in bed.

Clarissa pulled a soft blanket over the small child and placed a hand on her forehead. Despite her newfound cheerfulness, she still had a horrible fever.

Clarissa stepped outside the room to let her sleep, passing Tristan again on her way to the kitchen to wash dishes.

"Actually... can we talk about it?" he ventured.

Clarissa nodded, abandoning dishes for empathy, and sat on the floor beside Tristan. "Of course."

"You're going to miss Eloise's graduation," Tristan pointed out.

"Eloise will be okay. Right now, I'm here for you."

Jemma

Jemma could see Mistcoast on the horizon now, growing closer with every step. Her stubbornness kept her going. She could have stopped for one more night of rest, arriving tomorrow, but she pushed herself to the brink of exhaustion instead. Mistcoast was close.

She entered the outskirts of the town. For the first time in a week, she saw not just birds and trees and a deserted dirt road, but real buildings and real people. She headed down the main street of the town, with a weird feeling of belonging despite her hatred for the place. She felt an odd sense of joy until she noticed the flower petals lining the edges of the streets, the kids running around with hands full of daisies and mouths full of pastries, and the adults happily chatting amongst each other.

Jemma veered off the main path towards her old, abandoned treehouse. She couldn't handle the happy expressions and the joyful laughter.

They acted as if this stupid festival was a time for celebration and not for grief.

Part 4

The Anchors

Reece

Five years ago, in the middle of the spring festival, the town had been attacked. Pirates had heard of the apparently famed Mistcoast and came to steal the abundant riches, but the treasure was a myth, and Mistcoast was nothing more than a town of honest people trying their best to provide for their families. By the time the pirates realized this, it was too late. Some citizens fought back, others ran, and many died.

At least this was the version of the story Reece had pieced together from overheard snippets of conversations and drunken, tearful rants. He hadn't been present for the tragedy—he had moved to Mistcoast a few months after—but the festival became his busiest day of the year. Some people drank to celebrate, and others drank to mourn. Reece did neither. He simply cleaned dishes and wiped down tables after the opening night of the festival to prepare for the much busier day tomorrow.

Elijah

"Dad? Are you awake?" a small voice whispered in Elijah's ear.

Elijah rolled over to see his wide-eyed son staring at him. "I'm awake now."

"Can we go to the festival?"

"Sure, kid." Elijah rolled out of bed and found clean clothes for both himself and his son. He crumpled his son's clothes into a ball and launched it across the room, hitting his son in the back of the head.

Tobias laughed. "Dad!"

"Get dressed," Eli said as he put on his own clothes.

Once they were both ready, Tobias practically dragged Eli out the door. Eli was surprised by his eagerness. Just last night, Tobias had been hesitant to go to the festival—and given the history, Eli didn't blame him—so they spent the evening at Sophia's house instead. Today, Tobias walked straight into the festival. Crowds gathered in the center of the town. Live music bellowed from a band across the road. Flowers decorated the space, woven into garlands hung between buildings and arranged into pots that lined the walkways. Tables were scattered about with vendors selling bouquets and fruit-filled pastries.

Elijah shoved his hands in his pockets and followed his enthusiastic kid. He hated this place, but he'd gladly push that feeling aside for his son, who walked around the festival like a man on a mission in search of something important. After a few minutes, Elijah finally asked.

"What are you looking for, kid?"

Tobias turned around, giving his dad a look as if he had asked a stupid question. "Aunt Sophia."

"She'll probably be here later," Elijah told him.

"I want her to come now."

Elijah grinned. He was happy to see that his kid enjoyed spending time with his sister.

"She promised she'd buy me as many cherry pastries as I want," Tobias added.

Well that explained everything.

Half an hour later, to Tobias's excitement, Aunt Sophia showed up. She picked Tobias up on her back, bought him a pastry, and carried him onto the makeshift dance floor in the middle of the crowd. Elijah watched from the outskirts, occasionally waving at his joyful son each time the kid noticed him. Eventually, Sophia caught his gaze and danced her way back to her brother. Her eyes softened as she neared him.

"Do you want a moment by yourself to go to the docks?"

Eli looked at Tobias and then back at Sophia. "Are you sure?"

"Of course!" she said with a grin. "Me and the kid have this whole 'festival' thing figured out. Right, Toby?"

"Right!" Tobias shouted. "Can I have another cherry pastry?"

"One more cherry pastry, coming right up!" she said as she sauntered off with Tobias on her shoulders.

"Bye, Dad!" Tobias shouted.

Elijah waved goodbye before ditching the crowded festival. He walked along the docks, watching the boats sway gently on the waves. A few other stragglers hung by the ocean, but unlike the festival attendees, most sat in silence. One offered Eli a drink, but he turned it down. He didn't want to forget. He deserved the pain of her memory.

On the day of the attack, Eli's wife had disappeared, her body never found. Her boat had never been found either. The town assumed she was dead and comforted Eli the best they knew how. Eli never told them his theory: that she had taken the boat and left.

They'd been in a fight the night before the attack, another fight the week before that, and plenty of prior fights leading up to those. She had threatened to leave in the heat of an argument, but Eli never assumed she was serious.

He watched the horizon and imagined his wife in the distance, sailing away from Mistcoast on a journey to another continent.

He'd rather imagine that than her body at the bottom of the ocean.

Clarissa

Clarissa plastered a smile on her face and ushered the kids out the door towards the festival. It was hard to find a balance between comforting the kids who needed to grieve and reveling with the kids who loved Mistcoast's biggest celebration.

For the fifth year in a row, she pushed her own grief aside, trying her best to repress the memories of watching her dad die. She told herself it wasn't important, that remembering the evils of the past would only distract her from the good she could do now. That's exactly what her mother had done; she started an orphanage and adopted the 11 kids who had lost their family in the attack. In her grief, she found a purpose, a way to help people who needed her.

To Clarissa's surprise, in the morning, Abigail seemed to be in high spirits, and her fever had decreased. She still needed to see a doctor in Caridelle—the illness still concerned Clarissa—but it seemed that, for today, Abigail would be alright. After a lot of internal debate, Clarissa decided to leave Abigail alone for an hour and follow the other kids to the festival, swearing to herself that she'd keep the orphanage door in her line of sight at all times in case Abigail peeked out needing something. Clarissa could spend a bit of time at the festival on her last day with the kids before they moved to their new homes and she packed her bags for the capital.

All of the kids followed Clarissa to the celebration—even Tristan, to her surprise. Their conversation last night must have gone well. She had spent almost an hour listening to him recount his memories of the day.

They cried together over the tragedy, but Clarissa gave him permission to still enjoy the activities. Grief didn't necessitate sadness; it wasn't disrespectful to Tristan's parents for him to still enjoy an orange pastry at the festival.

She held Owen's hand tight as they walked towards the sound of music and laughter and the smell of flowers and baked goods. Clarissa bought nine caramel apples from a table set up just outside the orphanage and handed them out to the kids. She'd promised to split the remaining orphanage funds among the new parents who adopted the kids, taking for herself only what she needed to get Abigail to Caridelle and back, but the place was well-funded and a few caramel apples wouldn't make a dent in the budget.

Music spread through the air as a local band played. People gathered to listen and talk and laugh. The children weaved through the crowds, screaming with joy as they played their made-up games. Clarissa sat back and watched, trying to keep two eyes trained on nine kids.

"You didn't buy yourself one," a voice said. Reece handed her a caramel apple.

"Stalker," Clarissa joked, gladly taking the treat.

"Says the girl who knows everything about everyone."

"What are you talking about?"

"You keep track of what everyone needs at all times, Clarissa, and you read people like a telepath. I don't know how you do it."

"I'm not *doing* anything. I'm just living."

"And that's what makes it all the wilder," Reece said. "One of these days, you should let someone keep track of what *you* need." Without another ominous word, Reece disappeared into the crowd.

Clarissa chuckled at first and then gritted her teeth when she realized she had lost the nine kids in the commotion. She scanned the crowd. Charlette was with Mr. Ellis, and Cosette was standing nearby talking with Tobias. The teenagers were following Eloise and their friends around the festival. Clarissa fidgeted with her hair, searching for the remaining two. She found Tristan in a line to buy lemon tarts with his new dad talking his ear off and Owen climbing a tree with his new siblings. She sighed in relief. These kids would be okay without her.

Derek

Derek walked towards the fighting ring in broad daylight. It felt wrong. He was used to sneaking out of the house in the dark of night, being careful to move unnoticed, but now, he simply walked into the building. He didn't care who recognized him as long as Torin didn't see.

Tara sat at a table with Kane, eating a cherry pastry.

"Did you get that from the festival?" Derek asked. He was surprised Tara had visited the festival; she and Torin usually tried to avoid the celebration while also avoiding each other.

"Kane bought it for me," she said as she wiped cherry filling from her lips.

"I tried to get her to come with me, since she said Torin wouldn't be there, but she refused."

"Did you ask why?"

"I didn't push," Kane said.

Derek sat down at the table. "We used to have two more siblings: Thomas and Devin."

"There were *more*?"

"I'm not having that many kids," Tara said, looking at Alec, who lay sleeping on a blanket on the floor.

"Thomas and Devin were killed in the attack," Derek explained. Kane nodded in understanding.

"I was supposed to be looking after them," Tara said, staring down at her hands in her lap.

"You were thirteen. You shouldn't have been responsible for an eleven- and a nine-year-old," Derek reminded her. He'd said it again and again, but he could never fully convince her.

"I lost track of them," Tara mumbled. She lowered her head and tried to hide her tears, which only muddled her voice further until Derek could barely make out her words. "I was trying to find them when the chaos began. I found their bodies an hour later."

"It's not your fault," Kane said. He placed a hand on her shoulder.

"Derek tells me that all the time," Tara told him, "but I still hate the festival."

"We don't have to go then," Kane said.

"We'll have our own little party here," Derek assured her.

Tara chuckled. "As long as Torin doesn't find us."

"I don't care if he finds us," Kane said. "He'd be an idiot to not leave when Derek and I tell him to."

Tara chuckled again. "I thought you two were going to hate each other."

"We knew each other long before I met you," Kane reminded her.

"Does paying me to fight for entertainment count as 'knowing' each other?" Derek asked.

"Close enough," Kane said.

"Who would win if you fought each other?" Tara asked.

Kane gave Derek a look. "Do you want to find out?"

Derek grinned back.

Tara jokingly shoved them apart. "No! No fighting. I make the rules. Like you said, we're having our own little party here, a party all for me."

"I don't remember saying that part," Derek said.

"No, I'm pretty sure you said the party is all for her," Kane agreed.

"And I say we need more cherry pastries!" Tara decreed.

Derek rolled his eyes and stood up from the table, volunteering himself to retrieve the snacks. "Alright, I'll be back in a bit. Don't do anything stupid while I'm gone."

Jemma

Jemma woke up to broad daylight. Her familiar treehouse had allowed her to rest more comfortably than her makeshift camps on the road, and the crashing of the waves in the distance lulled her to sleep. Now, the music of the annoying festival called her awake. She rubbed her sleepy eyes and climbed out of her tree.

She didn't understand why people still liked this festival. It was the anniversary of her parents' deaths—and the deaths of a bunch of other people. Every year, while others celebrated the beginning of spring, she remembered the worst day of her life.

Jemma had never been good at listening to her parents. She hung out with friends that they didn't like. She never paid attention in class. She skipped school consistently, especially when they told her not to. She wondered what they'd think of her dropping out now, except she didn't really have to wonder. It was clear what they'd think.

She hadn't listened at all during the week leading up to the festival five years ago. She hadn't done any of her homework; she'd skipped school and snuck into a tavern. She'd stolen from the flower gardens grown for the festival. Her parents were fed up with it, and for the first time, actually punished her. Before then, it had been empty threats, promises that if she did it again, they'd do something. This time, they banned her from attending the festival.

She cried and cried when they left the house without her, leaving her alone with Sophia to babysit for a few hours. They'd visited the festival without their daughter, and now their daughter spent the rest of her life without them. They never came home that day. Around sunset, someone finally came, speaking to Sophia in a hushed voice. Sophia told Jemma the news. Eleven-year-old Jemma had been mad at Sophia for telling her the truth. Sixteen-year-old Jemma now knew better. There was no proper way to tell a child her parents were dead.

She couldn't fix it. Her parents were gone. There was nothing she could do to help them, but she could help her best friend, who was in danger now. She headed towards Reece's tavern. She needed to find some paper.

Jareth

No one in the town seemed to know what to do.

Jareth brought his mom to the festival and bought her some flowers. She hadn't remembered that today was the festival, but she was excited nonetheless. They strolled along the shoreline for a bit before wandering back home. Plenty of people were enjoying the festival, but there were many stragglers sitting on the beach or in their homes, thinking presumably about what this day signified in Mistcoast's history. To Jareth's relief, his mom was blissfully ignorant. If her memory was going to fade, the attack was a good thing to forget.

When they arrived home, the door was ajar. Jareth peeked inside hesitantly, holding his palms out, ready to cast a spell in self-defense. His dad smiled back at him. "Hey, kid."

"Hi!" Jareth's mom ran and embraced her husband. He'd only been gone for a month, but she hugged him as if he'd been gone for years. The family sat around the kitchen table together as Jareth's dad told of his adventures across the sea, stories embellished for dramatic effect. Jareth's mom showed off her bouquet from the festival and talked about all the sights she'd seen. Jareth waited impatiently. He wanted to talk to his dad alone, but he didn't want to steal his parents' time together. It took a few hours, but he finally got a chance to pull his dad aside.

Jareth took a deep breath. "Listen, Mom's memory is getting worse—"

"I know."

"—and I'm trying my best to take care of her—"

"I know that too."

"—but I know you'll leave again for another work trip soon, so I need some help figuring out—"

"Jareth." His dad placed his hands on Jareth's shoulders. "I'm not going anywhere. I told the crew that was my last trip. They've already found some new kid to replace me."

Jareth blinked in confusion. "Really?"

"I've been saving up to retire, and now seems like a good time."

Jareth sighed in relief. "That makes this so much easier. You can keep an eye on Mom while I'm at work, and I can help when I get home, so—"

"Jareth, I've got this. Look at me." His dad stared into his eyes. "I appreciate your help lately. I really do, but I've got this now. Don't worry about your mom. I'll take care of her."

Jareth paused. "Are you sure? I really don't mind helping when I'm not at work."

"Jareth, you did a great job while I was gone," his dad said with a proud smile. "Now go live your life, kid."

Jareth shook his head. "What else am I supposed to do?"

"I don't know. You're nineteen. Go do something stupid. Go travel the world." His dad grinned. "Go ask out that girl."

"She's leaving town tomorrow."

"Then you have tonight," his dad said. "Seriously, go back to the festival. I'll stay here with your mom."

"I can't just leave."

"Sure you can. We'll be fine. We'll play some card games." He let go of his son's shoulders. "Go be young."

Jareth rolled his eyes as he walked off. "I love you, Dad."

"I love you too, son."

Elijah

After sitting in silence alone for a while, Elijah left the docks and walked towards the busy center of town. He had needed the time to himself, but he didn't want to abandon Tobias all day. He searched through the crowds but couldn't find his son or his sister. After asking around with no success, he decided to try Sophia's house, and sure enough, there she was, sitting outside the small home.

Eli waved as he approached. "Why'd you come home?"

"Tobias wanted to take a nap," Sophia explained as she stood up. "I think his stomach hurts. He probably ate too many pastries."

"Why did you buy him so many, then?"

"I'm his aunt," she said with a smile. "It's my job to spoil him."

Elijah sat in the empty chair beside his sister. "I... I need to tell you something, and you're not going to like it."

"Did you lose the boat?" she asked.

He turned his head to stare at her. "How did you know?"

"I heard from Reece, who heard from Cohen, who felt terrible about it."

"I can't believe you found out so quickly."

She shrugged. "You should be used to it by now. It's part of living in a small town."

He sighed. "I tried my best. I caught as many fish as I could. I took as many extra jobs as Cohen would give me."

"It's okay."

"It's not okay. I have to feed my kid."

"I'm not going to let him starve, okay? He's your kid, but he's also my nephew. I'll take care of him."

"I need a new job," Eli mumbled, frustrated.

Sophia nodded. "You need a new job *soon*."

"Yes, Sophia, soon. I'm aware."

"I don't want you waiting around forever. Take the first job you can find."

Eli sighed. "I have to figure out something that still lets me pick up Tobias after school. He's not old enough to stay home alone."

"If that becomes a problem, then he can come with me after school. He can sleep here if he has to. Take the first job you can get, okay? We'll figure out the details later."

"I don't want to have to rely on my big sister."

Sophia gently pulled him in for a hug. "I've been relying on my little brother my whole life. I can't even kill a spider on my own."

"That's different, Sophia. This is my kid. I should be able to take care of him."

Sophia let go of him and took a step back to stare into his eyes. "I know your pride doesn't want you to ask for help, but get over it. It takes a village, Elijah. Let me be the village."

Jareth

Jareth wandered through the festival looking for Clarissa. To his surprise, she was nowhere to be found, yet the kids were here running around with their friends. He wasn't sure what to do. Reality had begun to sink in, and he decided this might be a bad idea.

Sure, he'd had a crush on Clarissa since the beginning of secondary school, but it was nothing but a crush. He hadn't actually ever planned to ask her on a real date. His dad used to say that crushes fade, that Jareth was too young to know what he really wanted in a girl. Now, he was old enough to know, and either his younger self knew too or had a lucky guess. The butterflies in his stomach that appeared every time he saw her at school never faded; they just morphed into something different, something more mature. Teenage infatuation turned into an honest appreciation for Clarissa's kindness and empathy, and his self-centered dreams of dating her were replaced with a genuine love and care for her well-being.

Looking around the festival, he didn't see Clarissa, but he found Eloise hanging out with the other new graduates. He paused a few yards away. He didn't want to interrupt, but Eloise noticed him watching and turned her attention. "What's up?" she asked.

"Do you know where Clarissa is?"

"She probably went to check on Abigail. Why?"

"No reason. I'll stop by the orphanage."

"Have fun." Eloise returned to her conversation as Jareth walked off.

With a box of lemon tarts in hand, he knocked on the door of the orphanage. He waited patiently. There was no response. He knocked again, but nothing happened.

He walked to the side of the building and peeked in a window. Abigail's door was ajar.

This was a horrible time to ask out this girl. It was the anniversary of her dad's death, and she was busy caring for a sick child. Who was he to bother her at a time like this? He took a step back from the building and looked down at the lemon tarts in his hands. Maybe this was a bad idea, or maybe this was exactly what Clarissa needed to make her bad day a little better. He'd never know until he tried. Besides, Clarissa would head to Caridelle tomorrow. This was his last chance.

He opened the unlocked front door and immediately paused. He heard crying, then an almost guttural scream. His frozen state turned into running, and he burst into Abigail's room.

Collapsed on the floor was Clarissa, holding a limp little Abigail in her arms. Clarissa stared at Jareth in terror and sorrow, her face bright red and covered in tears.

Jareth knelt beside her and placed his hand in front of Abigail's face. He couldn't feel her breathing.

"Go get Derek," Clarissa said almost inaudibly between shaky breaths. She spoke with no sense of hope, only an obligation to try. Jareth ran out of the building to help in the only way he could.

Derek

Derek took a deep breath. "Clarissa..."

"Don't say it." She curled up into a ball, leaning against Jareth.

"Clarissa. Look at me."

"No." She buried her face in her knees, her tears dampening her skirt.

"She's gone, Clarissa."

"No!" She screamed, and Derek watched as Jareth pulled her closer.

There was nothing Derek could do. No amount of medicine and bandages could bring someone back from the dead.

"I'm sorry, Clarissa."

"You were supposed to make her better, Derek!" Clarissa yelled. "You gave her medicine! You told her she'd be okay!"

"I did everything I could," Derek said calmly.

"Get out!" Clarissa yelled.

Jareth looked between Derek and Clarissa, unsure of how to break the tension. Derek laid Abigail in her bed and pulled a blanket over her face. He stood up and stepped towards the door. "I'll leave."

"Wait," Clarissa mumbled. "I'm sorry. I didn't mean to yell at you."

"It's no big deal," Derek said, and he meant it. Clarissa, the nicest person he knew, yelled at him in a moment of grief. It was nothing compared with the anger and screaming he dealt with on a regular basis.

She looked up at Derek and then at Jareth as she leaned away from him. "I just... I just need a moment alone," she said before disappearing into her room.

They waited until nightfall, until the crowds of the festival had dispersed to their homes, to carry little Abigail out of the orphanage to the cemetery hidden in the back of the woods. Bit by bit, Derek dug into the dirt, his muscles fueled by the rage in his veins. Jareth watched with tears in his eyes. Clarissa didn't watch at all. Derek buried little Abigail beside her parents.

Clarissa gently laid a bundle of flowers on top of the fresh mound of dirt. "She wanted me to bring her these flowers from the festival," Clarissa said quietly. "She never even got to see them."

Jareth knelt beside Clarissa and placed a gentle hand on her shoulder. "She would have loved them."

They waited in silence, minutes that felt like hours, until Clarissa stood up to leave. Derek and Jareth followed her cue and walked with her back to the orphanage. "Do you want one of us to stay with you?" Jareth asked as they reached her home.

She shook her head. "No, it's... it's okay. I'll be okay." She nodded. "I'll be okay. I just need some sleep," she said as she walked into the orphanage. Derek heard the click of the lock on the door.

"Are you going to come check on her in the morning, or do I need to?" Derek asked Jareth.

"I can do it," Jareth said as he hesitantly pulled his gaze away from the door. "Are you going home now?"

"I need to go check on my sister," Derek said with a sigh. In the dark of night, he left Jareth behind and walked towards the fighting ring.

"Derek! What took you so long?" Tara teased as he walked in. "You're so slow. You—" She paused abruptly when she got a good look at his face, and her tone shifted to one of sympathy. "What happened?"

"I had to bury a body," Derek mumbled, which sent Tara into a panic.

"What? Who? How did—"

"Abigail," he said quietly.

Tara paused and took a deep breath. She watched her brother's sad eyes, letting the silence permeate for a minute before speaking in a whisper. "I'm sorry."

"Who's Abigail?" Kane asked cautiously as Derek sat down at the table.

"A little girl who never even grew old enough to learn to tie her shoes."

Tara looked down at the baby in her hands, who was giggling in blissful ignorance. Derek reached over and touched Alec's palm, and the baby gripped his finger tight. Tara leaned her head on her brother's shoulder and stared into Alec's eyes with tears in hers. "Life isn't fair."

CLARISSA

In the dark of night, the girl clutched Abigail's toy rabbit to her chest and cried herself to sleep.

Jareth

As the sun began to shed light on Mistcoast, Jareth knocked on the door of the orphanage, fighting his eyes to stay open. He had barely slept the night before; his worry wouldn't allow it. When Clarissa answered the door, it was clear she had slept even less than he had.

"Oh. Hi." She rubbed her tired eyes. "Here, come in," she said, holding the door open for him.

Jareth stepped inside, and Clarissa closed the door behind him before immediately heading towards the kitchen. "You're probably hungry, right? What do you like for breakfast? I'm not really hungry, but do you like omelets?" She reached for a carton of eggs, almost dropping it in her tired state. As Jareth followed her into the kitchen, she turned around suddenly to look at him with wide eyes. "You're not allergic to eggs, right? I don't want you to die... or starve..."

Jareth stepped towards her and took the eggs out of her shaking hands. "You don't need to worry about cooking me anything."

"But you need to eat breakfast," Clarissa argued.

"Claris—"

"Breakfast is the most important meal of the day."

He froze for a second, unsure of how to respond to the stubbornly kind girl, before he grabbed an orange off the counter. "Breakfast. See?" He held up the orange to show her, then peeled it.

"That's not a balanced meal," she argued, but she stepped out of the kitchen in surrender. She took a slow, shaky breath as she looked around the living room. Jareth had never seen the place so clean, so quiet. He watched Clarissa gasp for air, tears forming in her eyes.

"Clarissa," he said cautiously, taking a step closer. "Let's go for a walk."

She nodded slowly and reached for his hand. Jareth led her out the door of the orphanage. They passed the playground and the school and the market with no particular destination in mind, just a need to keep moving.

Jareth looked down at their hands intertwined, her grip so tense that her knuckles turned white. He had always imagined the day he got to hold this girl's hand, but he never imagined it like this.

"What's that?" Clarissa whispered, her first quiet words spoken since they had left the orphanage. She pointed at a piece of paper nailed to a tree. Jareth walked closer to read it.

"I need help with a quest! Traveling to Illia and then Caridelle to return a stolen treasure. It'll take a week or a month or something between there. The quest will pay lots. Meet me at Reece's at sunset two days after the festeval."

Clarissa shrugged numbly. "I was already planning on going to Caridelle."

Jareth shook his head. It was her choice, but now was not the time to be making decisions. "Why don't you think about it for a bit first?" He took the flyer off the tree and carried it on their walk.

They took their time with their morning tour of Mistcoast. Jareth led them through the less busy parts of town to avoid familiar faces; he had a feeling even well-meaning friends may be the opposite of helpful right now.

As they neared the orphanage again, Jareth noticed movement through one of the windows. He beat Clarissa to the front door and opened it slowly.

"You left the door unlocked," Derek said. "What's that?" he asked, pointing to the note in Jareth's hand. He grabbed it to read before Jareth had a chance to answer. He paused in silence, reading it over several times, then sighed.

"What?" Jareth asked.

"I could use the money."

"I want to go," Clarissa said.

Derek looked up at her. "You could use a distraction."

Jareth looked between Derek and Clarissa. Were the two of them seriously considering this?

Normally, Jareth would have shut down the idea. They were just random teenagers from a small town; this was way out of their realm of expertise. Besides, even if they left, Jareth couldn't go with them. He couldn't just leave his parents behind. Could he? His dad *had* told him to "be young" and "do something stupid" and "travel this world". He glanced back at the flyer. This sure seemed to meet those criteria.

"We should at least take a couple of days to think about it," Jareth said.

"You're considering going too?" Derek asked. "Don't you have a job?"

"I don't care about that," Jareth said. He'd much rather go on a quest with the girl he liked than try to please a boss he hated.

Elijah

Eli sat on his bed with the flyer in hand. Sophia had told him to take the first job he could find. This probably wasn't what she meant, but Elijah didn't care. He had already asked around for other jobs and hadn't gotten a single lead. This, albeit not ideal, seemed pretty guaranteed.

He stepped into Reece's tavern and saw a table of people holding the same flyer. He instantly recognized Jareth, Clarissa, and Derek.

"Which one of you wrote this?"

"You didn't write it?" Jareth asked.

Elijah shook his head.

"I guess we'll have to wait and see," Clarissa mumbled. She stared at her hands clenched tight on the table. Something was wrong, very wrong, but Derek continued the conversation before Eli could even think of what to ask.

"Do you think we'll have to fight someone on this quest?" Derek asked.

"Not everyone needs to be punched," Clarissa told him.

"I don't have to punch everyone. I have a bow too."

"I have a sword," Elijah said. He hadn't thought much about it until now, but maybe his father's sword would be useful. Maybe he'd come home with as many crazy stories of adventure as his dad had.

"I know some magic," Jareth said.

They all turned to look at him. "When did you learn that?" Clarissa asked.

Jareth sighed. "It's a long story."

"You should teach me," Clarissa said. "I don't have any weapons."

"I'm sure we won't need to fight anything," Elijah assured her. "I'm sure it'll be easy."

"The note didn't say anything about needing experience," Jareth said.

"Well, it also didn't spell festival correctly," Eli pointed out. "Seriously, who wrote this?"

"You'll find out soon," Reece said as he approached the group. "Knowing her, she'll be late. In the meantime, what do you want to drink?"

Jemma

Jemma walked towards Reece's tavern excitedly. She was about to meet her team, assuming people showed up. She assured herself they would. They had to. She needed to save Callum, and she needed their help to do so.

She burst through the tavern doors with a grin on her face. "Hi, everyone!" She froze when she noticed the group of people, scanning each of their faces and quickly evaluating.

The guy from the fighting ring was good at, well, fighting. He'd be useful.

Then there was the guy from the boat she'd tried to stowaway on. Hopefully, he wasn't still mad at her.

Jareth was there too. She didn't particularly like him, but she didn't hate him either. He could tag along.

The biggest surprise of all was Clarissa. Jemma frowned. She didn't like this.

"You wrote this?" Clarissa asked.

"Yes."

"Is it real?"

"I don't lie," Jemma said. Clarissa's eyebrows raised. "Well, I wouldn't lie about this at least," Jemma clarified.

"She's telling the truth about this one," Reece told Clarissa.

Jemma nodded in agreement. She didn't like Clarissa, but she needed people, and Clarissa would be helpful whether Jemma wanted her to be or not. "So, are you on board?" Jemma asked.

An interrogation ensued; her team had an obnoxious number of questions. She answered most of them truthfully. She only left out two things: that the quest came from a thieves' guild, and that they were doing it to save Callum. Those details weren't important to them anyways, she decided. She told them everything else.

After a lot of debate and discussion, they all agreed to go. Jemma grinned. Reece gave her a thumbs-up.

This was her team. These were the people who would save her best friend.

Elijah

Elijah sat on his bed, looking down at the flyer with tears in his eyes.

"What's that, Dad?" Tobias asked as he pulled his pajama shirt over his head.

"It's a job, Tobias. It means I'm going to have to leave for a little while."

"For a day?" Tobias asked.

"For a few weeks," Elijah said, watching carefully through tearful eyes for his son's reaction.

Tobias didn't scream or cry or argue; he simply hugged his father tight. "Where will I go?"

"You'll stay with Aunt Sophia. She'll take good care of you."

"You're really going to leave?"

"Yes, but I'll come back," Elijah said. "I promise you I'll always come back."

Tobias pulled away from his dad and lay down in bed. He tugged the blanket up to his chin with a sad smile. "Goodnight, Dad."

"Goodnight, Tobias." Eli kissed him on the forehead and started to walk away.

"Dad?"

"Yes?"

"Can you sing me that song?"

Elijah took a deep breath. He couldn't say no to his kid now. He returned to Tobias's side and sat on the edge of the bed, running his fingers through his son's hair as he sang for him Anna's lullaby:

If you were a cloud, then I'd be your sky
If you were the ocean, I'd sail through the night
If you were the stars, then I'd be the moon
'Cause I love you, I love you, I do

If you were a bird, then I'd be your nest
If you're ever tired, then I'll be your rest
If you're ever lost, then I'll be your route
'Cause I love you, I love you, I do

If you ever need me, then I'll be right here
So close, little eyes, there's nothing to fear
Now sleep, little child, the day will come new
'Cause I love you, I love you, I do, I do
'Cause I love you, I love you, I do

Acknowledgements

The Mistcoast Misfits is, first and foremost, a story about family in all its forms. I couldn't have written this book without the family that surrounds me.

Mom, Dad, Alyssa, Tyler, and Tyler: thank you for supporting me in my crazy and wild dreams of becoming an author. I love you all more than I can express.

To my musician and beta reader, David Scherm, thank you making this lullaby come alive. I could have never imagined that we'd progress from leading a tiny worship band to recording and releasing music together.

To my artists, Lydia Jordan and Jordan Frimpter, thank you for using your beautiful talents to give readers a picture of the small town of Mistcoast.

To my alpha readers—Avery Hudgeons, Zech Roberson, and Sydney Short—thank you for seeing this story in its messiest form and believing in it nonetheless. This book has come so far since the first draft you read, and it wouldn't be what it is today without your help.

To my beta readers—Simon Meyer, Justin Heard, Ian Tate, and Audrey Villanueva—thank you for all of your excitement and edits. I mean it when I say that out of all the authors on the planet, I have the best team of beta readers.

Lastly, I want to thank UTD for giving me a place to edit, to thank Duck Tales (you know who you are) for dragging me to campus to write, and to thank that one bag of chips—our favorite bag of chips—on the side of the road.

And of course, I thank God for the ability and freedom to use writing to express the many thoughts and emotions He's given me.

About the Author

Tessa Marie is a full time data scientist and part time author, dedicated to writing intriguing and inspiring stories across a variety of genres. When she's not writing code or books, she enjoys playing guitar, spending time with friends, and repeatedly losing to her husband in video games. Follow her writing journey (and other adventures) on Instagram: @tessa_marie_writes.

www.ingramcontent.com/pod-product-compliance
Lightning Source LLC
LaVergne TN
LVHW090513110826
845146LV00003B/837